MAXIMUM JOY

A NOVEL

BONNIE AND RICH VANNUCCI

Origin Press
in cooperation with
Operation Serving Children

Origin Press
www.OriginPress.org
PO Box 3364
New York, NY 10027

Jacket design by The Book Designers
Interior design by Carla Green (claritydesignworks.com)

ISBN: 978-1-57983-059-5

Printed in the United States of America

First printing: October 2019

Acknowledgments

This story has been a big part of our life for decades. Thanks to our friend, editor, and publisher, Byron Belitsos, it has finally all come together in this novel. His guidance and wisdom steered us in amazing directions. The never-ending encouragement that he offered kept us motivated. Most of all, his special spirit and belief in our mission has brought us all closer to the goal of spreading the spirit of sharing throughout the world. Thank you also to the Origin Press creative team for the explosive cover artwork and book design that truly represents joy.

Many friends and family members have heard us talk about our story for many years. We thank them for listening and for their kind words of encouragement along the way. We especially thank our children: our son Pablo, a creative author in his own right, who graciously came to our rescue by helping us tear down the writing blocks that got in our way, and who is also our video producer and social media director; our son Marco, who shared his marketing and digital arts skills in creating our new websites; and our daughter Nina, who has been our constant supporter and our number one fan. They have grown up with this story and we are thrilled that they are part of this mission.

None of this would be possible without the love of our Creator, as well as the special bond of love between the two of us that we have been blessed with. We have travelled a long and joyful road, and are truly thankful for every moment of this journey.

Dedicated to our parents who taught us
about the love of our Creator,
our children who are proof of the love of our Creator,
and future generations who will benefit from the
better world that we will create together.

Joy is strength.
—Mother Teresa

"What am I doing here?"

Nic mumbled to himself as he began to cross the intersection. He could barely breathe. Sweat rolled down his face and dripped into a sea of human despair. He paused on the curb and stood motionless amid the chaos. His throat felt scratchy from the soot kicked up from the trucks and buses. Enormous bulls sauntered through as if they were royalty. The streets were so crowded it was hard for Nic to see even a few feet ahead. Families squatted in little pockets along the sidewalk. Nic could see a child vomiting near him and heard a woman giving birth just a couple of steps away, but what he saw directly in front of him stopped him in his tracks.

God, this can't be real!

Nic beheld a screaming, naked newborn lying alone in the middle of the busy intersection. Unfazed, a large white Brahman bull stepped over the child, almost crushing it. He felt a tug on his sleeve. It was Carlos, his host in India.

"Nic, what's wrong?"

Nic lifted an unsteady finger. He pointed to the baby.

Carlos spotted the baby and placed a consoling hand on Nic's shoulder. "It's all right Nic, stay here. I'll be right back."

Nic wasn't listening to Carlos. Nic was already working his way to the infant, dodging the crowd like a skilled football player making his way to the end zone. Taking off his shirt, Nic stooped and gently wrapped the baby. He made his way back to Carlos.

"Nic, there is an orphanage just two blocks away. Follow me."

Nic bounced back to reality. He looked at the tiny baby in his arms. "Who is this?" he asked as he cooed to the infant. "Why did they leave her there?"

Carlos responded, "It doesn't do us much good to ask why. We must only ask what we can do about it."

They turned into an alley ending with a large gate and a wall surrounding a tall building. Carlos rang the bell. An elderly woman emerged from the building and opened the gate promptly, greeting the unexpected guests. "Carlos, what have you been blessed with?"

Nic handed over the bundle and retrieved his shirt.

"We just found her. Actually, Nic did."

The woman smiled at Nic. "Thank you, young man. I hope you realize the importance of what you have done. You have saved a life today." She noticed Nic's pale face and trembling hands. "You've never been here before, have you?" Nic nervously shook his head. The woman smiled at the baby and looked back at Nic. "Welcome to Calcutta."

* * *

NIC WOKE UP the next morning and rolled over on his thin, lumpy mattress. He was staying at a university with Carlos, who was in charge of the leprosy colonies that an American charity had established far from Calcutta in a rural area of the state of Bihar. Carlos was a longtime friend of Nic's family and had been working in India since 1972, rarely leaving India for the past eleven years. He had invited Nic to join his newly assembled 1983 team of volunteers, knowing Nic would be a good fit.

Nic could hear the noisy crowd that hadn't left the streets all night. He shuddered as the vision of the bull stepping around the helpless infant flashed through his mind.

Just a few weeks ago, Nic's surroundings had been far different. He was working on his Master of Divinity degree at a large American university. Although Nic's spiritual connection was deep and his aspiration to be a preacher and teacher was strong, his desire to minister to those who were suffering was even stronger. He was tired of second-hand theology; he wanted to actually serve others in need.

Nic sat up, trying to shake off a stinging sensation in his arm that had woken him. As he rubbed his hand across his swollen arm, he jumped out of bed in panic. Large red welts covered it from his elbow to his wrist. *Great.* he thought to himself. *First night here and I've already caught some kind of disease.*

"You don't have a disease. And there are other things you should be focused on."

Nic jumped, startled. He spun around, expecting to see Carlos. No one else was in his room. *Wonderful, now this disease is making me hear things.*

Nic still didn't see anyone. It seemed like the voice was coming from the far corner of the room. He squinted into the darkness. "Hello? Is someone here?"

"Of course there is. I'm always here."

Nic gasped in astonishment as a tall, stately man stepped out of the shadows, making Nic forget his arm. Spellbound, Nic noticed his long, golden hair, striking blue eyes, and rugged face. The mystery man radiated strength, poise, and peacefulness. He wore a long crimson and blue robe that seemed to wave and flow slowly as if it were under water. Nic had never seen him before, but he had an odd feeling the man wasn't exactly a stranger. "Who . . . who are you? Did Carlos send you?" Nic blinked a few times hoping it would clear his mind, but the figure was still there. *Am I hallucinating?*

The man grinned. "Carlos wasn't the one who sent me." He pointed to Nic's swollen arm. "You are complaining about your arm."

Nic quickly looked down at the blistering welts. "Uh, yeah. I just arrived, and I'm sure I have some kind of disease. Part of me knew I shouldn't have come here."

The man raised an eyebrow. "And what about the other part?"

Nic sensed that the stranger knew what he was about to say. "The other part of me needed to come here."

Nic quickly realized he still had no idea who he was talking to. "You never answered my question. Who exactly are you?"

"My name is Michael. Your name is Nic."

"How do you know my name?"

Michael clasped his hands together. "Nic, I know everything about you. I am an archangel."

"An archangel? Really?" He didn't look like an angel to Nic.

"If you're an archangel, then I'm Santa Claus," Nic said sarcastically.

"Agreed," nodded Michael with a friendly smirk.

The pain in Nic's arm had vanished. Nic was riveted on this outlandish figure who claimed to be an archangel. He was amazed and curious, but somehow not afraid. Michael exuded an exalted serenity that filled the room and calmed Nic.

Michael continued. "I have been assigned to you since before you were born. You, Nic, have been given two great gifts: the ability to see me, plus my availability to assist you. Even when you don't see me, I am right there beside you to guide you along your way. I support you in your special life mission along with the aid of other angelic helpers, including your two guardian seraphim who attend to the details of your everyday life. Nic, the Creator needs your help to rekindle the spirit of sharing in humankind."

Nic was flabbergasted. "My special life mission? The Creator? Help rekindle the spirit of sharing?" Nic repeated Michael's words skeptically. "What do you mean? What makes me so special?"

Michael knelt down and gingerly took Nic's swollen arm. "You are concerned about your survival, yet you have food to eat, and you live in comfort and safety."

"But my arm," Nic said quietly. Michael's gentle touch soothed him. "This is not what I signed up for."

"Ah, but it is," hummed Michael.

Nic looked up at the man. He still couldn't believe his eyes, but Nic was becoming intrigued by this talk of a supposed mission. "It would be great if I could rekindle the spirit of sharing, but how would I do that? How could anyone do that?"

Nic thought about the chaotic world of suffering beyond the fence surrounding the university. He flashed back to the image of the baby left alone in the street. *If humankind allowed something like that to happen, maybe humankind couldn't be helped. Maybe the world can't be fixed. Maybe it doesn't want to be.* Deep in thought, Nic considered for a moment how his theological training had been futile. "Maybe God should just give up on us."

Michael's eyes widened with surprise. "Do you really think the Creator would give up on the very children he made?"

"After seeing what I did yesterday, I probably would," Nic responded, shrugging his shoulders and feeling befuddled.

Nic watched as Michael knelt to the floor. The majestic archangel bent over and began to slowly trace a large circle on the floor, following his finger with his eyes. "What are you doing?" asked Nic as his eyes became fixed on a circle Michael was drawing.

Michael ignored Nic's question. The circling finger began to leave a trail of sparkling dust. Nic was mesmerized. A hologram shot up and magically came to life inside the circle on the ground before him. Nic watched in awe as a colorful sequence of scenes unfolded before him as Michael began to speak again.

"From the depths of Paradise and since the dawn of time, God our Creator has shared His gifts of life and love throughout all creation. The Creator has always dwelled in eternity with the high beings of Paradise who reside in the eternal central universe, but His infinite love moved Him to set into motion the material worlds and all the precious creatures that live on these whirling spheres of time and space."

Michael's voice now took on a tone of authority and grandeur. Nic listened and watched the stream of moving images, awestruck.

"The Creator's spirit-filled breath also poured forth to create the planet Earth. It all began as virgin stars collapsed and erupted into supernovas. From this raw material a plentitude of increasingly complex forms of matter condensed and became the stars of our galaxy. These elements eventually formed every mineral, plant, and animal that arose on Earth. And, it was all very good."

A tear came to Nic's eye as Nic caught Michael's allusion to the biblical creation story, but now updated with the language of science.

"Out of the wondrous diversity of life that arose on Earth, a species of incomparable worth arose that was endowed with the Creator's own image and spirit." Nick was breathless as he watched the procession of images that led up to a beautiful couple standing beside a primeval river. It reminded Nic of Adam and Eve.

"This special creation is, of course, humanity—God's only creatures with the ability to determine their own eternal destiny by making those personal choices that contribute to the growth of an immortal soul."

Michael paused and glanced at Nic. Nic's eyes were fixed on an image of the interior anatomy of a human figure, showing points of light. The archangel continued.

"As a child of God, every man and woman possesses within them an actual fragment of their Creator, a pure spark of God's own essence, a spirit that guides them and fosters the evolution of their soul. Impulses to love, share, and care for others flow forth from this divine spark into each human mind. Its inspirations can lead them to have faith in the Creator."

Now the scene changed and became a profusion of unique geometric patterns that seemed to descend from on high, like a swarm of divine snowflakes.

"The Creator also endowed each one of his children with a unique personality that gives them the power of free will and the ability to seek union with God. So important is humanity to our Creator that he created angels and other celestial entities who invisibly guide and teach each man and woman on Earth."

The peaceful series of scenes of celestial beings came to a halt, and the picture darkened. A different set of images paraded before Nic.

"But throughout the millennia, as humanity has exercised its gift of free will, things have not always gone well. Outside influences corrupted them. All too often, humans were misguided to make choices to please their own selfish egos while ignoring their subtle inner nature that quietly urges them to love one another. As a result, wars have raged, and hatred and greed have dominated Earth for eons. The Creator was greatly moved, so he sent a Son to heal and teach us. And, Christ's superb teachings and his matchless life brought a great light of hope and salvation to the world. Humankind has progressed quickly ever since, in fits and starts, but it still has a long way to go."

Nic nodded in full agreement.

"Today, because of fear and greed combined with poorly made decisions, your world's problems are becoming overwhelming and it is time for a new intervention from on high. Far too often, women, men, and children suffer from preventable disease and starvation. Climate change is becoming ominous, and there are wars and rumors of war. Refugees are flooding across borders in many places. A powerful few own almost everything, and billions live in dire poverty."

Nic stood up quickly. He felt like running from the tragic scenes Michael was displaying in the hologram, but he couldn't remove his gaze from the circle as the intensity grew.

"But now the end of this age is occurring." The chaotic series of events on Earth melded into a swirling image of our galaxy as if seen from above. Michael continued, his voice elevating with each word. "It is time to turn selfishness into selflessness and redirect this world towards its destiny in light and life. So, the all-merciful Creator has issued the mandate to begin what the angels call the 'Correcting Time,' the divine plan to rekindle the spirit of love and sharing on Earth. This is the very same spirit that Jesus brought to Earth two thousand years ago. But now it must be refashioned to suit the needs of your scientific age."

Michael's finger stopped. Nic found himself standing next to Michael in a wide-open space. He could see nothing but soothing white light all around them. Nic was filled with an indescribable peace. "Where are we?" questioned Nic softly.

Michael responded, "Do you know who Saint Nicholas is, Nic?"

"Yes," replied Nic confidently. "He is the first Santa Claus. My mother named me after him because I was born on December 6th, Saint Nicholas Day. When I was young, she told me that she believed I was destined to be a bearer of many gifts just like Nicholas." Nic smiled at the memory. "I was so excited when she told me that if God wills it, and if I work hard enough, I could grow up to become a great gift giver, a true Santa Claus."

"You are right, Nic. Nicholas is the original Santa Claus, but he was, and is, so much more."

Michael walked slowly into the source of the light and Nic followed him closely. "What do you mean?"

"Nicholas was a noble teacher of God who lived on Earth many centuries ago. He was very disappointed in the selfishness of humanity. During his life on your world, Nicholas was graced with the ability to embrace the spirit of our Creator, offering God's love and care to all he met by sharing all he had. Now he looks down upon Earth from the afterlife as an ascending spirit, sadly observing the strife and suffering that has continued down through the centuries on his world of origin."

Nic couldn't begin to imagine how difficult it must have been for Nicholas to watch so much travail for such a long time. What he had seen in Calcutta and in the brief holographic history that Michael had just shown him was disturbing enough.

"Nicholas was deeply concerned and even heartbroken," Michael continued, "so he enthusiastically joined with the angels and many other ascending humans like himself as a minister and teacher of the Correcting Time. And he was assigned a special task."

"What did the Creator ask Nicholas to do?"

"He was invited to form a singular mission in his mind, one in which he would probe the hearts of humanity, searching for those individuals gifted with the desire to serve through sharing. The Creator led Nicholas to envision a time when the right leaders would step forth, together, to become a powerful force in the building of the Kingdom of the Most High on Earth."

Michael paused. In the distance Nic could see a cloaked silhouette looking up into the light.

"Who is that?" Nic asked. "What is he doing?"

"You don't recognize him?"

Nic looked again. The figure had his arms outstretched, reaching up towards a blazing light. A red velvet cloak draped over his head and arms. Something about him seemed very familiar, but Nic could not see his face. "No. Should I?"

"That is who you are named after."

Nic's eyes widened with excitement. "That's Nicholas?"

Michael nodded.

"What's he doing?"

"Nicholas is boldly approaching the Creator with the details of his special mission idea, a plan that will foster the spirit of sharing and caring for those less fortunate."

Nicholas started to bellow towards the light. "It is time to release celestial teachers from the higher worlds to recruit those humans ready to accept the call to correction and transformation. I am ready to take up my own role within the Correcting Time as the Creator wills it to be."

Suddenly Nic felt the loving and awesome presence of the Creator. He was overwhelmed, and wept.

"Loving Creator," began Nicholas, "I know that you are deeply concerned about the condition of the planet Earth." Nicholas paused as a deep glow vibrated in his spirit, confirming the Creator's agreement. He raised his arms reverently. "I beseech you, oh Lord Creator, to send forth a mandate for rekindling the spirit of sharing among humanity as one strand of your beneficence flowing into the Great Correction!" Raising his face and closing his eyes, he announced boldly, "It is time!"

A bright, golden light surrounded Nicholas. Then, from above, three brilliant stars of emerald, ruby, and sapphire descended swiftly upon him. He remained motionless as the stars encircled him rapidly, surrounding him with a swirl of sparkling colors.

Michael whispered to Nic, "His request was granted. Three high angels—the spirits of generosity, hope, and courage—began a journey to Earth."

Nic watched now as Nicholas lowered his arms and opened his eyes. All was quiet. He bowed with humble appreciation for the Creator's mercy. "So be it. Once again, great Lord, you will guide humanity into a higher destiny with a new wave of grace as only your immense love can do."

Nic looked quickly around him. "What's happening? Where is Nicholas?" He was gone.

Michael spoke quickly. "The three powerful spirits jettisoned through the higher worlds in their descent. They soon joined the host of other celestials patiently awaiting their authorization to teach and lead humanity. The archangels hurled toward Earth, filled with the Creator's gifts of generosity, hope, and courage. As the planet whirled majestically through space, the spirits approached its surface and converged at the North Pole. Their impact propelled spirals of colors that formed into crystals like fireworks."

A sudden loud explosion made Nic jump. Michael put his hand on Nic's shoulder. "The crystals encompassed the planet, carried forth by the magnetic field of the earth. Soon the crystals reached their intended destinations. Each one found a place to settle within all those who were ready to accept the spirit of sharing. One by one, these special jewels of improved character were absorbed by charitable individuals of all the races and nations. One crystal approached and entered the heart of a boy in a small town in Pennsylvania."

The scene instantly changed. Like a distant echo from the past, Nic heard a boy yelling, "There is too!" A very familiar scene flashed before him. Nic saw a young boy being pushed into the snow by two bullies. The victim's mouth was wide open, yelling his protest as his face was being pounded with snow. Nic recognized where he was standing. It was the schoolyard in Williamsport, Pennsylvania where he grew up. It was all happening so fast that he almost missed the flash of light approaching quickly from above. It was one of the crystals. It descended with great speed, colliding with the bullies' victim. Nic felt a warm sensation spreading through his body. The memory of that day was clear. It was the day when the Lucci brothers humiliated him because Nic insisted that Santa Claus really existed.

The boy started choking and the bullies released their grip. He sat up quickly and yelled, "There is too!" Coughing, and still feeling their choke-hold, he asserted, "I know it is . . . true! Ahh!" He yelled as his face was pounded with snow again. The bullies laughed.

"How did you get to be so smart?" they teased.

"I *know* it's true!" the boy insisted as he squirmed away and jumped up, shaking the wet snow from his hair.

"What? That he's real? And just how?" one of the brothers bellowed, planting his fists firmly on his hips as the crowd of students around them got larger and louder.

"I'm named after him," the boy said confidently. He continued to brush the snow from his covered body and stood still in anticipation of the next attack. Although he could possibly defend himself by fighting back, he would not, could not do so.

I didn't believe in violence and fighting, thought Nic as he watched his nine-year-old self become an easy target. The bully clenched a tight grip on the boy's right arm.

"Ouch," exclaimed Nic, grabbing his right arm.

Something switched and Nic sat up. He was in his bed at the university in Calcutta.

Nic breathed heavily as he looked at his swollen arm. Then he glanced around the room. Michael was gone. Nic sat still for a moment, his rapid breath beginning to slow. He was back in the humidity of India.

Nic joined Carlos for a simple breakfast in the university kitchen. He felt withdrawn and puzzled, unwilling to discuss his bizarre encounter. Carlos noticed Nic's swollen arm. "Do you know what happened to your arm?" he asked Nic, assuming his ailment was what was distracting Nic.

Nic shook his head, bringing himself back to the present.

Carlos put his hand on Nic's shoulder. "Looks like you slept with your arm up against the mosquito net. You'll learn to sleep in the center of the net from now on. We have just the cream to help soothe that."

Nic knew he had a lot to learn to survive in this very different world.

"Ah, there you are," said Carlos, his attention turning to the doorway. A young man, a bit younger than Nic, slowly stepped into the room. His clothes were worn but kept neat, and a faded blue ball cap rested firmly on his head.

"Nic, this is Joseph," said Carlos as he approached the young man. "He will be your escort to Bihar. Joseph is familiar with travels through this area and will make sure you get to your destination safely." Carlos smiled at him and gave his shoulder a firm pat. Joseph smiled.

"Nice to meet you Joseph. I'm Nic. Thank you for taking the time to be my escort."

Joseph stood motionless and continued to smile. Nic recognized Joseph's blank look. "He doesn't speak English, does he?" he realized.

"No, he doesn't," replied Carlos, "but he is very patient and will try his best to understand your needs. You'll be fine."

"Everything is an adventure around here, isn't it?" said Nic with a slight sigh.

"Yes, my boy, it sure is." Carlos smiled at Nic with the loving smile of a father to his son. "It is time for you to gather your things and head for Bihar. They are looking forward to your arrival."

I bet they're looking forward to it more than I am, thought Nic with an uneasy feeling as he returned to his room to get ready. But he felt something else too. He now understood why he was so driven to be like Santa Claus. *It's inside of me. It's who I am. Even if I don't like where it takes me sometimes.*

Nic boldly picked up his backpack, thinking about Michael and Nicholas. "I am ready to fulfill my mission," he announced out loud, unaware that his mission was very far from being fulfilled.

Life doesn't have to be perfect
to be filled with joy.
—Anonymous

Nic, Carlos, and Joseph arrived at the train station shortly before the scheduled departure. Nic panicked when Carlos informed him that he would not be joining them.

"I guess you didn't get my last letter about the assignment," was Carlos' response when Nic questioned him. "You have a 12 to 15-hour train ride to Gomoh, a city in the state of Bihar in north-central India. You will be acting as the administrator of our leprosy colony there, standing in for its director who is leaving for a three-month visit back home to the States. You will be replacing him for the first six weeks, and another volunteer will arrive just after you leave to run things for the last six weeks. Your presence will ensure that the children's schools in our leprosy colonies will run as usual."

Carlos continued to explain that simply having one "Westerner" there would keep everyone in line and allow things to operate without a glitch. "Everyone in the colony, from students to teachers to cooks, are former leprosy patients," he said. "They're very grateful for the gift of a new life and will work hard as long as they know you are there for them."

Nic followed Joseph, unable to avoid bumping into the stream of people hurrying past him. He was glad they would not be spending much time at the station. *This crowd seems to follow me everywhere*, thought Nic as he once again got pushed through a jostling throng of noisy people. He tried not to show his disgust at the strong smell of unbathed bodies. Unfazed by the odor and the congestion, Joseph moved quickly through the crowd, trying to open a path for Nic to follow. "I guess you have to get used to it," mumbled Nic to himself. "I wonder if I'll ever get used to it."

Nic continued to play follow-the-leader until Joseph stopped abruptly at the edge of the platform. Nic took a spot close to him. People continued to press into him as they claimed their spot on the platform, waiting for the train. Nic looked at his feet. The platform was made of rickety, worn wood. The wooden planks shifted unsteadily with the movement of the crowd. A train slowly backed into position, its steel frame rattling furiously, adding to the already deafening noise of the train station. The train jerked as it came to a stop at the platform with a loud grinding squeak.

The crowd began to move toward the train. It filled quickly. Nic purposely sat next to a window but was now wondering if that was a good idea. The windows were wide open and covered with wide-set bars instead of glass. Although they let in much-needed air, they also let in all of the surrounding dirt and noise. Many still crowded on the platform, pushing to get onto the train.

"Where are they all going to sit?" Nic asked Joseph, not expecting an answer. "Are they all going to stand? There isn't enough room."

The crowd continued to board the train, filling every vacant space to be found. They sat on the floor of the aisles and even between the seats by other passengers' feet. Nic found himself being pushed closer and closer against the window. He was now very glad he chose a window seat as the passengers sitting at the aisle had to deal with people practically sitting on their laps.

I guess these people have never heard about invading someone's personal space, thought Nic.

When he sat down, he placed his larger bag on the floor at his feet with his backpack on his lap. Nic decided it was a good strategy as he now had foot space.

Nic tried to turn his body to look around the train, but he could only turn his head and shoulders slightly. From what he could see, the train was more than full. He looked out the window and saw even more people on the platform approaching the train. He still had no idea where all of these people were going to sit.

A sudden loud barrage of thuds above his head answered his question. The remaining ticket holders climbed up to sit on the slightly arched roof of the train. There were no rails or straps for support. They balanced and braced themselves for the bumpy ride.

"If I had to ride like that, I would ask for my money back," Nic whispered to himself. The commotion on the roof unnerved Nic. "In fact, I think I would probably forget this whole trip."

He jumped to the jerk of the train as it began to move along. Leaning his head back, he closed his eyes. His thoughts went where they always seemed to go: *Sara*. Nic hadn't seen Sara since he was nine years old, yet she was always in the forefront of his mind. He couldn't figure out why; it was just a natural part of him.

Nic returned to his fond memories of the girl. They met early one morning when he was on his way to school. He had often walked by Sara's house but rarely saw her. That morning he discovered her hanging on a bar suspended from a swing set in her front yard. Two feet of fresh snow surrounded her. Nic found himself stopping to watch, spellbound by her agility and her joyous laughter. He was so mesmerized by her smile, long brown hair, and her deep brown eyes that he barely noticed that she had a weak, withered arm that dangled at her side.

As Nic watched, the little girl attempted a spin-off from the swing. She landed feet first but then fell forward into the snowbank around the swing. She started laughing despite her awkward spill, and Nic found himself chuckling out loud along with her. His laughter drew her attention, and she called out to Nic to join her. She jumped back onto the swing, grasped the chain with her good hand, and started a new swing.

Nic started towards her but stopped. The snow was almost waist high. He looked up at her swinging, unsure about the snow piled up around them. Sara convinced him that it was the best time to swing because the snow would break a fall. Enthused by her invitation, Nic started plowing through the snow. Together, they shook the snow off the vacant seat. It took a bit of energy to get the first few swings going amidst their giggles, but they finally got up high enough for their feet to swing up above the mounds of snow below them. They laughed harder and louder as they swung higher and higher, stretching their legs and pointing their toes hard, trying to touch the dancing flakes that had begun to fall. They shared a feeling of maximum joy as if they had known each other forever.

Their revelry was interrupted by Sara's mother who suddenly darted out of the house and firmly instructed Sara to go inside. Her mother explained that Sara wasn't wearing a coat and could not be outside in the cold without one. When Nic asked if she could come back out to play after she put on a coat, he was shocked when her mother lowered her head and said with teary eyes that Sara did not have one. They did not have money to buy one. Nic was perplexed. His family worked very hard for very little, yet they always had money for everyone to have jackets. He could not understand how someone could not have money to buy something as simple as a coat. Not long after that day, Sara's mother remarried and the family moved to Florida. Since then, throughout the years, Nic had been unable to shake Sara from his thoughts.

Images of Sara as a child and what she might look like now often popped up in the window of Nic's mind. His vision of her was so clear. She was dressed simply in khaki pants held by a wide belt around her slim waist, plus a tan shirt and a thin orange scarf. Her long dark hair was tied back loosely; several loose pieces hung freely, framing her pretty face. Nic remembered her smile that so warmed him on that cold winter day, as well as his determination to get Sara a coat. *Dad was so embarrassed when he found out I borrowed money from relatives to buy that coat*, chuckled Nic to himself. He thought about how upset he was when he was sent to his room and was unable to deliver the package to Sara. He was then even more upset and afraid to tell his father that he had lost the package with the coat. He was grounded, so it wasn't until after Christmas vacation that he saw Sara again. He was surprised to see her wearing the coat he had gotten her. He could still hear the excitement in her sweet voice when he asked her where she got the coat.

"I woke up Christmas morning with the most beautifully wrapped gift next to my pillow. The wrapping was shimmering like crystals, and the bow glowed like real gold. There was a note that read, 'To Sara, from . . .'"

Nic remembered finishing her sentence. *To Sara from Santa.* He smiled, thinking about the sparkle in her eye as she pressed the palm of her hand to his chest and whispered, "Great things can happen if we just believe."

It seemed like nothing could ever separate us, sighed Nic almost out loud, reliving the joy he felt as they ran together for the swings. Sara's announcement just a few weeks later that they were moving to Florida broke Nic's heart, but throughout the years he experienced deep feelings for her.

Suddenly, the train jerked fiercely to a stop, throwing Nic's things around and startling him to his senses. "We can't be there yet, can we?" he asked Joseph who was still sitting in the same slumped position that he had settled into when they began their journey. Joseph was sandwiched tightly between Nic and another passenger, barely able to move. Nic leaned his head out of the window. He saw a cow standing placidly on the railroad tracks. Before he could react to the unusual roadblock, his attention was drawn back inside the train by the sound of a female passenger on the other side of the aisle yelling in disgust. The young mother swiftly unwrapped her infant and hung her out the window, holding her firmly by the waist, as the baby finished urinating. When finished, the mother methodically shook the infant dry and re-wrapped her. The mother sat back down expressionless, nuzzling and cooing her baby.

A bit stunned by the event, Nic leaned out the window once again. The cow slowly ambled off the tracks, and the train started moving again with a jerk. Nic wiggled back into his space, trying to appear unimpressed. He glanced over at Joseph who seemed to be frozen in time.

What's so sad, thought Nic, *is that they become so immune to this. They have no choice. This is their life.* He endured the rest of the trip in silence, frozen in time with Joseph.

Hours later, the train wheezed and jerked, coming to a stop at the main station in the far interior of Bihar state. The sights, sounds, and smells at the Bihar stop were much the same as at the station in Calcutta—unruly crowds of people filling an old wooden platform. He clutched his belongings tightly and awkwardly stood up to depart the train. Joseph got up and nodded to Nic to follow him. As they moved slowly down the aisle to the door, Nic passed the young mother and her baby. Nodding towards the baby, Nic smiled. The mother's large dark eyes met Nic's uncomfortably for a moment. She glanced down at her baby and then her eyes returned to Nic, this time with a soft sparkle. It was the first faint sign of joy that Nic had seen since arriving in this overwhelming land.

Nic and his escort disembarked the train and pushed their way through the crowd. Joseph yelled something to a boy standing by a rickshaw taxi. The rickshaws were everywhere. Their owners were yelling to pedestrians passing by. After an exchange between Joseph and the boy, Joseph and Nic climbed onto the rickshaw. The young barefoot boy picked up the handles and started to run in the mud. They traveled uphill on a muddy road passing hordes of destitute people. Nic admired the young boy's strength, agility, and focus as he pushed his way through the throngs. He only lost his footing once or twice, his bare feet sliding in the mud as if he was climbing a mountain with patches of ice.

As they approached the top of the hill, Nic saw a compound consisting of six or seven rectangular, one-story cement buildings, each with many doors. "Is this the school?" he asked Joseph, pointing up the hill. He looked at Joseph, pointing to himself and then to the buildings. "I am going there?" Joseph understood Nic's gesture and affirmed his suspicions with a sideways nod and a smile.

They arrived at the hostel—a school for former lepers. Nic would soon learn that five hundred children ranging from age three to eighteen plus a staff of cured lepers made it their home. The children had all been afflicted with leprosy, an airborne virus common among societies that endure a lack of nutrition, poor hygiene, and a hot, humid climate. Leprosy attacks the central nervous system, destroying the victim's sense of touch. Because of this lack of sensation, the patient is unaware of injury. Often, hands are burned in a fire, or open sores on the bottom of their feet are ignored. Infection sometimes leads to gangrene and the loss of digits or limbs. In addition, the cartilage of a leper usually deteriorates, causing deformities. The characteristic flat nose, droopy ears, and short fingers of a former leper mark them for life. The children at the hostel had all been cured of the virus but were not welcome back in their villages. Their deformities were so misunderstood that they were banished from family and society.

The boy pulled the rickshaw to the middle of the complex, and they came to a stop. Nic jumped off and looked around at his temporary home. The hostel was situated at the top of a hill and surrounded by large beautiful trees. The park-like setting was a contrast to the simple, plain cement buildings. Although the grounds were all dirt, the area had a neat, clean appearance to it. The lepers, having been forced out of their towns, took it upon themselves to create their own village. It was obvious to Nic that they took pride in their new home.

The entire school was there for Nic's arrival. As he entered the compound, the crowd closed in on him, cheering and chanting, and greeting him like a hero. Without warning, a group of young boys ran up to Nic and jumped all over him. He suddenly remembered Joseph. "Joseph!" Nic turned his head just in time to see Joseph being pulled away in the rickshaw, heading back to town. There was a part of Nic that wanted to yell, "*Wait, take me back with you.*" Instead, he managed to raise his arm to wave his farewell and thanks. Joseph responded with a quick wave and a smile.

An older, rough-looking man worked his way up to Nic, shooing the excited boys away. He was short and stout, and his confidence made it obvious that he held a position of authority. He held out his hand to welcome Nic with a handshake. With his other hand, he made a fist and held out his thumb, pointing to himself.

"Uncle," he said. "Manage school."

It took a moment for Nic to interpret the few words of broken English, but he finally understood. Nic took Uncle's hand and gave it a firm shake.

"Nic," he said introducing himself. Uncle turned towards a young girl standing next to him. She was dressed in a brightly colored sari with worn strap sandals on her feet. "Sabina, girl's camp," said Uncle as he pointed across the road.

Sabina eagerly stepped forward to greet Nic. With hands held together in prayer and a wide smile, she bowed. "Namaste. Welcome, Nic."

Nic bowed in return. "Yes. Thank you. You know English?"

Sabina bowed again. "A very little, yes, and you?"

Nic laughed. "Yes, I too know a little." Sabina took his arm and led him through the crowd, which was still cheering at Nic's arrival. "What a welcome."

Sabina smiled. "It is a great day when the children get visitors, especially from America."

Nic guessed Sabina was no more than twenty years old. Her long black hair donned the sheen of youth, and her lips were plump and shiny. Although her skin was weathered by the hot sun and dry air, she had an innocent quality about her that gave away her young age. She led Nic to one of the cement buildings. "You already met Uncle. You may go to him for anything, but Uncle knows very little English. The rest of the people here know only their own language, Hindi. Uncle usually spends his time in the village, but when he is here, he can help you." They approached a doorway with a small porch hosting a battered metal folding chair at its threshold. Sabina pulled back the thin blanket hanging in the doorway and motioned to Nic to enter. "We can talk more later but as for now, it is almost time for dinner. Let me show you your room." Sabina led Nic into a large, bare room. There was a thin mattress sitting a few inches off of the floor with a blue mosquito net covering it.

"What do the other doors of this building lead to?" asked Nic.

"They all enter the classroom," replied Sabina.

A young boy entered the room, carrying Nic's bags. He set them down, walked over to Sabina, and motioned to her to lean over. He whispered into her ear. Sabina lightly covered her mouth to hide her giggles. Standing up, she looked at Nic. "He has heard you have a Western toilet here; he would like to know if he may see it."

Nic looked at her with eyes wide. "He wants to see my toilet? What does he mean by 'Western' toilet?"

Sabina looked seriously at him. "Here, we all use the field beyond the last building. Men on right, women on left. I'll show you later."

"That's okay," Nic interrupted. "No hurry for that tour. Let the boy go ahead and have a look."

Nic was given a quick tour of the hostel on the way to dinner, although the now-familiar sulfur smell rising from the coal stoves hampered his appetite. Students and staff followed the neatly swept dirt paths around the grounds in an orderly fashion. The children were happy, their eyes bright, and big smiles filled their faces as they enjoyed their camaraderie. *This is so different from the India that I saw in Calcutta.*

Concrete buildings were spread throughout the compound. Nic's room was in the building at the compound's center. The dirt paths that connected each building were surrounded by an occasional bush or hedge. Nic and Sabina took a path to the right of Nic's room that led to two buildings.

"These two buildings are the classrooms for the boys. They also serve as dormitories for the children," pointed out Sabina.

"Where do the girls attend class and sleep?" asked Nic. Sabina turned around and pointed to two buildings on the other side of the compound. They were positioned just across a narrow road behind a low gate that separated them from the main compound.

"Those are the girls' classrooms and dormitories. The girls and boys attend school and sleep separately, but all other activities are together."

They continued to follow the dirt path behind the center building. They approached another set of two buildings. "This is the tailor building." Sabina opened a creaky metal door to reveal a large room filled with rows of sewing machines manned by children who were being taught to sew. "This is a valuable skill that offers a student the opportunity to become a tailor and earn a living making and altering clothing. They are not allowed to hold a job in the town, but work is brought to them. If they are very fortunate, they sometimes leave here to work in villages that understand their affliction and can accept them. In these cases, the school gives them a sewing machine, and they start their own tailor shop."

The sound of the machines echoed in the busy room. It was lit by dim lights hung by flimsy wires dangling from the ceiling that cast a shadow across the workspace. *How can they see in such bad lighting*? The children looked up one by one, staring wide-eyed at Nic. He nodded his greeting as Sabina led him out and motioned to Nic to follow a stony path.

Just behind the tailor building was the welding workshop. "Other students learn metal work, another valuable skill," explained Sabina as they approached the building. The sound of powerful equipment banging on metal clanged from the building. Nic and Sabina looked in the window.

"What are they working on?"

"There is an open abandoned well on the other side of this building. The students are forming a lid to be placed on the well to seal it."

"Impressive," exclaimed Nic, admiring the concentration and skill of the students. He noticed a few of them wiping beads of sweat from their foreheads as they worked.

As they strolled further along the path, Nic admired the tall trees within the compound. "What's back there?" He pointed to a field behind the welding workshop.

Sabina's voice was proud. "Those are the rice fields where we grow our rice."

The fields consisted of large rectangles of wispy green grass standing six to eight inches high, placed methodically throughout. Each rectangle was bordered by a frame of wood and was filled with water. Nic estimated that the area was about the size of a football field. Children and adults donning burlap pouches with straps draped across their bodies littered the field. Each worker was bent over, either gathering rice or pulling weeds.

Nic and Sabina now entered a large outdoor pavilion that functioned as the kitchen and dining area for the compound. The sulfur smell became stronger as Nic came upon a thick stream of smoke pouring from the soft brown coals used for cooking. The smoke was so rancid that it almost brought Nic to the point of nausea. With classes now coming to an end, everyone was gathering for dinner. The crowd stopped their conversation to cheer Nic's arrival. All of the attention was starting to make Nic feel like his mission wasn't going to be so bad after all.

3

Sometimes your joy is the source of your smile,
but sometimes your smile can be the source of your joy.
—Thich Nhat Hanh

Nic looked around. Big dark eyes beamed at him, framed by faces of brown weathered skin, their big smiles accentuating leathery wrinkles caused by the sun. Loose skin rippled across their small, thin bodies topped with striking ash brown hair. The girls wore their hair long, draping over their plain white saris, and the boys donned a short, neat cut matching the proper look of their white shirts and cotton pants. Although their clothing was washed on the rocks in the river, their outfits looked very crisp and clean.

Nic got in line and was given a large, firm banana leaf. Rice was scooped on top of it from one of several large pots of boiling rice. Nic looked around and saw that there were no other food options. Plus, there were no chairs, tables, or utensils. Sabina escorted him over to a clearing in the center of the area. Everyone continued to stare at him.

As Nic waved to his gazing audience, he became increasingly self-conscious. "Why are they all staring at me like this?"

"We have had only a few Westerners visit. But you are the first with hair of gold."

"Hair of gold? We call this color blonde."

Sabina tried the new English word. "Yes. Blee-ond." She squatted down and gestured for Nic to do the same. With much difficulty he squatted down over the ground, trying not to fall over. Slowly bending his knees, he lowered his buttocks onto his calves. He felt as if a slight breeze would knock him over. He held the leaf in his right hand and began to eat with his left. Nic looked up and noticed to his surprise that the hundreds of children's eyes were still fixed on him. Unable to ignore them, he noticed their facial expressions turning from smiles to disgust as they murmured to each other and pointed at him. He quickly stopped chewing and swallowed with a gulp. He looked at Sabina. "What's wrong?"

"You are using the wrong hand to eat," Sabina whispered. "Switch hands."

Nic quickly moved to hold the leaf in his left hand. "Is that better? I'm sorry. I don't know your customs."

Sabina responded sternly. "It is no custom. It is hygiene. We eat with our right and wipe with our left. We do not eat with the left."

"Wipe what?"

Sabina giggled and shook her head. "That I will explain later, after dinner."

Nic thought for a moment and finally understood. "Oh, you mean it has to do with the field? I now know why Carlos said to bring TP with me."

Sabina stopped eating and looked at Nic. "TP? What is this TP?"

Nic smiled. "I'll explain that later too." He picked up a handful of rice with his right hand, confident of his utensil choice. "This rice is delicious."

Sabina sat up and smiled. "I am pleased you like it. It is good that you do. We have it for breakfast, lunch, and dinner every day."

Nic was shocked. "Every day? You can't be serious?"

Sabina stood up. "Come. We will finish eating as we walk. The sun will set soon. As we get little more than two hours of electricity a week, all go to bed at dusk. We rise at sunrise. I want you to get settled before dark."

They started walking across the complex toward Nic's room. Nic looked around at all the children. There were so many. As they walked to his room, children ran up to Nic, excitedly touching his arms, legs, and head. He looked at Sabina. "They want to touch the hair of gold," she said with a smile. Nic didn't mind. It was such a pleasure to see smiling faces after witnessing so much misery.

As they continued to stroll across the compound, Nic felt as if he was being followed. Behind him was a young boy trailing him and smiling uncontrollably. It was the boy who had asked to see his toilet. He was small and thin, his large dark eyes accentuated by short, neat dark hair. "Who do we have here?"

"This is Raja," Sabina said. "He was found when he was an infant and brought to us. The people are uneducated, and in their ignorance they believe that an infant inflicted with leprosy has sinned in a previous life and is being punished. Such a baby is taken to the woods at the end of the village and is left to die."

"Abandoned, just like the infant we found in Calcutta," mumbled Nic to himself. Nic squatted down in front of the boy. "Would you like to join us on our walk?"

Sabina translated. The boy's eyes sparkled as he nodded his head with a definite "yes."

Nic offered the boy his hand, who gripped it tightly, walking proudly next to his new golden-haired friend. "Where do the children sleep? I don't see any beds."

Sabina pointed to the buildings around them. "On the floors in the classrooms."

Nic was appalled. "But they're all cement."

Sabina glowed. "Yes, isn't that wonderful? It is so much nicer than the dirt the children are accustomed to, and they each get a blanket."

Raja skipped alongside Nic. His joy made Nic feel special. They approached the porch in front of Nic's room.

"Thank you for your visit here," smiled Sabina. "Sleep well tonight. Tomorrow will be full of many surprises."

Nic bowed. "Goodnight and thank you so much for your help." He let go of his little friend's hand and bowed his good-bye. Raja returned the bow and ran off across the complex to join the other children who were now out playing after their evening meal. Nic noticed that the children weren't playing with toys. He couldn't locate one ball, jump rope, or doll in their play area. That didn't stop them from running, laughing, and screaming with delight.

Nic entered his room and unpacked a few things. There was no dresser for his clothes, just a simple wooden four-legged table next to his bed, so he laid his clothes on top of his bag. He neatly arranged the rolls of toilet paper along the wall and crawled into the bed tucking the mosquito netting around him, holding a notebook and flashlight. The thin bed was unexpectedly comfortable with soft white sheets and a frayed blanket. Sabina had told him that he had the only bed in the school. He remembered with amazement how proud she was that the children slept on cement and not in the dirt. Nic entered his updates in his journal, shaking his head continuously as he recalled the almost unbelievable events of the day. Closing the notebook, he set it at the foot of his bed. A bit stunned, he laid back down. Nic rubbed his arm. He still had a few small welts from the mosquito frenzy during his stay with Carlos. He made sure that his mosquito netting was secure this time and positioned his arms tucked under his sides, away from the net. "How has Carlos been able to handle staying in Calcutta for so many years?" he wondered.

A strange noise caught his attention. He pointed the flashlight to the wall. A three-foot-long lizard clung to the wall near the door, staring at Nic as if he were the intruder. Nic sighed and tried to go to sleep. He remembered what Sabina said. "Sleep well tonight. Tomorrow will be full of many surprises."

"What else would I expect but surprises?" chuckled Nic to himself. He listened to the lizard scurrying along the wall, hoping that it wouldn't come near him. He yawned loudly. The long train trip and the excitement of the day had been exhausting. He rolled onto his side and thought about his encounter with Nicholas and Michael. *I don't think anything will surprise me anymore*, he thought, drifting into a peaceful sleep.

"Life is full of surprises, Nic."

Nic had fallen asleep so quickly that he didn't see Michael appear at the foot of his bed.

"You're unaware of surprises that have shaped your life. But you can dream them back to your awareness." Michael waved his hand over Nic, "Remember Nic. Remember when…"

Michael looked on as the young Nic held the railing and hung sideways from the top of the stairs while peering through the banisters. Nicholas was delivering gifts under the tree. Much to his delight, Nic thought he saw a shiny blue bike resting next to the tree. Stretching to see more clearly, he lost his balance and tumbled down the stairs. He rolled uncontrollably and found his momentum stopped by a wall of soft red velvet. Nic looked up at the towering figure.

Nicholas looked down with a smile and started to laugh quietly. "Well, what have we here?"

Nic rolled away quickly and bounded to his feet. Nicholas stood tall, draped with a flowing red velvet robe. A loose red hood covered his head, exposing a frame of long, white, wavy hair around his face, melding into a thick white beard that cascaded like a waterfall past his shoulders and across his chest. Between his nose and his upper lip lay an impressive mustache that curled across his puffy pink cheeks like the wings of a dove. Thick white eyebrows adorned his eyes, accentuating dark star-shaped pupils floating in a blue-green sea. In his right hand, he held a majestic wooden staff that seemed to glow with a life of its own. It was inlaid with shiny glowing orbs of red, blue, and green.

Nic looked up and was mesmerized when he saw what was nestled inside the curl of the staff. It was a wooden carving of the heads of three children. The intricate artwork was impressive, portraying every detail as if it were a photograph. The carving had been painted with meticulous detail, adding a life-like quality to the trio. Their cheeks pressed firmly against each other as if they were one. Nic took a half step forward, keeping his eyes on the staff.

Nicholas realized Nic's fascination. He slowly leaned the staff forward. Nic took a bold step closer, examining the carving. As he inspected the trio, their painted eyes began to sparkle with the mischief often seen in the eyes of Nic and his friends when they played games of make-believe. Then, much to Nic's surprise, the children smiled at him and giggled.

Nicholas leaned the staff back to its proud position by his side. The eyes of the children no longer sparkled. Having returned to their painted splendor, Nic moved his attention back to Nicholas when he spoke.

"Nic, I know you have been teased for your belief in me. I share your frustration regarding people who are mean and selfish and who do not believe. You think they don't treat you well? Look how they treat me. I've become a clearance sign for special sales, a tasteless television show, and embarrassing movies." His tone was agitated. He took a deep, calming breath. "There is strength in being meek and humble, Nic. We can care for each other compassionately with a quiet strength that is stronger than a thousand men." Nic's attention followed Nicholas as he strolled around the room, his eyebrows still furrowed. "Nic, it's time. I need your help."

"You need *my* help?"

"Yes, Nic. I need your help to rekindle the spirit of sharing in humankind." Nicholas smiled with confidence.

"Rekindle the spirit of sharing? What's that?"

"Show people that the true spirit of Santa Claus is *sharing*." Nicholas leaned back, awaiting Nic's reaction.

"Okay," Nic replied absentmindedly.

Nic looked past Nicholas and eyed the bright blue bike that Nicholas had placed carefully next to the tree. The sight of the bike disrupted the conversation as he brushed past Nicholas to the bike. It was spectacular, exactly what he had dreamed of. Nicholas' plea for help left his mind. "Is this bike for me?" he asked with a distinct tone of hope.

Nicholas smiled. "Seems to be the right size and isn't this the color you asked for?" He reached down and helped Nic onto the bike. "Yes, just the right size indeed."

Nic started riding around and around Nicholas, the tree, and the gifts, smiling a smile of great joy. But as he swerved to miss a large box wrapped in red-and-white-striped paper donning a large red bow, the sudden movement forced him to brush past the tree, knocking down an ornament. It shattered as it hit the floor. Nic turned to look at the broken glass ball, briefly lost his balance, and bumped into the tree. The tree teetered for a moment. The ornaments swayed and clanked as if crying for help. Then the tree suddenly fell to the floor with a crash. Oblivious to the mess, little Nic continued to circle Nicholas and laughed. Nicholas held up his staff. The trio of children adorning the curling hook came to life, laughing along with Nic with joy, their laughs creating a shower of fine gold crystal dust that streamed out everywhere.

"Ho, ho, ho!" bellowed Nicholas as he waved his staff, directing the golden cloud.

The gold dust started to whirl around Nic's head. Sparkles of red, blue, and green brightly shimmered within it, making Nic dizzy and his eyes heavy. He tried to ride harder and faster as the room swirled and spun.

Nic woke abruptly to find two big watery eyes looking curiously at him. He rolled to his back, startling the lizard. Nic watched him scurry back to his spot on the wall. Staring at the ceiling he pondered, *I knew I saw Nicholas somewhere before. I always remembered the bike, but I didn't remember him asking me to help him. It didn't make sense back then.* Nic rolled back to his side and breathed deeply. "But now I understand," Nic whispered. "I will try to help you Nicholas."

* * *

A BATHROOM WITH A SINK and toilet was a luxury that Nic was thankful for. He leaned over the basin and turned on the faucet. A cistern on the roof collected the rainwater that was piped down to the faucet in his bathroom. He was the only one there who had this system, which was built for the pleasure of their Western visitors. He splashed the lukewarm water on his face. It was hardly refreshing on a hot day, but he didn't dare complain. It was far better than bathing in the river, which was what everybody else did.

Nic headed to the dining area to have breakfast with everyone. As usual, Raja joined him, walking hand-in-hand. Nic smiled as the boy tugged rhythmically on his arm when he started to skip alongside him. Nic wasn't sure why, but he felt a special connection with this boy. *Maybe it's because of the way that he followed me on that first day*, pondered Nic. Raja giggled as Nic awkwardly tried to skip alongside him. Nic couldn't help but giggle too. *He's a sign of hope*, thought Nic. *A hope that someday all people will live knowing the joy of Raja.*

Raja began to repeatedly shout a word among his giggles. "Faster? You want me to go faster?" Nic found it hard to find the breath to speak. He was slowly learning the Hindi language and Raja's word was one that he understood. He tried his best during conversations but usually stumbled to the delight of the students who often laughed at him when he spoke. He wished he could speak Hindi fluently so that he could talk with Raja. Nic knew there was so much he could learn from the young boy.

They reached the dining area. Nic breathed in deeply to catch his breath as he took his place in line with a banana leaf. He felt fine until they plopped the usual pile of rice onto his leaf. Suddenly, he felt a queasiness overtake him. "The skipping must have shaken me up," Nic said to himself. He paused and looked away, taking a few deep breaths. He followed Sabina to their usual dining spot under a Bodhi tree and squatted. As soon as he looked at the rice, he felt strange again. Shaking his head, he ignored the feeling and joined in on the conversation.

"What a nice, dry day," said Nic, trying to take his mind off of how he felt.

"Yes," replied Sabina. "It is going to be cold like this for some time." She noticed Nic wasn't eating. "Nic, are you going to eat?"

Nic adjusted his squat. "Yes, I am." Reluctantly, he looked down at his rice. The first handful was hard to swallow, and the second was even more challenging.

Sabina looked over at him. "Eat, eat. It is time to go to the classrooms soon."

Nic looked over and smiled as he gathered another handful of rice. As his hand rose to meet his mouth, he unexpectedly started to vomit uncontrollably. His violent vomiting finally ended, leaving Nic weak, dizzy, and unable to walk. An illness was creeping up on him, claiming his body as its own.

Nic couldn't eat for a few days, his stomach convulsing each time rice was offered to him. Even the mention of rice or the mere sight of it caused him to begin dry-heaving.

"This is the worst flu bug I have ever had," he moaned as he lay in his bed, feeling miserable. "I just need to stay in bed. It will go away in a couple of days," Nic assured Sabina as she did her best to keep him comfortable. Her look of concern and quiet demeanor puzzled Nic. *The people here are sicker than this,* thought Nic. *It's nice of her to take care of me, but why is she taking this so seriously?"*

Raja checked on him several times each day, hoping Nic would get well enough to get up for their routine walks around the compound. Although Nic didn't want Raja to catch his flu, his joyful smile soothed him. "If you stay by the door and don't come too close, you can stay for a few minutes," he conveyed to Raja in his broken Hindi, shooing him back if he began to get too close.

Nic quickly got tired of being sick. "I have to get out of this bed," grumbled Nic. He found the strength to get out of bed and tend to his duties, going about his work visiting the classrooms and touring the grounds. Sabina stayed close to Nic, following him throughout the day. She was by his side as he sluggishly dragged himself around the grounds, taking many breaks and keeping to himself as much as possible. Nic still wasn't eating, and his obvious declining energy concerned Sabina.

"Deliver this note as quickly as possible," she told a messenger. The note was to be hand-delivered to Carlos in Calcutta. She felt it was imperative for Carlos to know about Nic's condition and his inability to eat rice, the only food that they had to offer him. "Carlos will send you what you need to eat so that you can regain your strength." Sabina explained to Nic as she continued to follow him through the compound.

"I hope it arrives soon." Nic stopped, swaying as if the ground was shifting below him.

"Nic, do you need to sit down? I will help you."

Nic shuffled his feet, attempting to walk. His eyes blurred as he collapsed to the ground, losing consciousness.

I slept and dreamt that life was joy.
I awoke and saw that life was service.
I acted and behold, service was joy.
—Tagore

Sabina broke his fall the best that she could, shielding his head from hitting the concrete. Her cry for help was quickly answered and Nic was promptly carried to his bed while a doctor was summoned. Raja followed closely behind, stopping in the doorway of Nic's room, his smiling face replaced with one of fear. Nic lay shaking and sweating, murmuring sounds they could not understand. The doctor turned to Sabina.

"Malaria," he announced.

It was no surprise to Sabina; she saw it often. Malaria. The word echoed in her head as she looked back down at Nic shaking under the blue mosquito net. Because there was no medicine available, Sabina could only watch her friend suffer. Hours passed before the shaking subsided. Nic fell unconscious, his muscles spasming periodically.

The doctor returned the next day. Closing the mosquito net around Nic, he turned to Sabina. "He has gotten through the worst," he informed her. "As the fever goes down, he should slowly regain consciousness."

Delirious images raced through Nic's head as he became partially aware. He saw the faces of the malnourished children of Calcutta looking at him, their oozing eyes disturbed by flies. Among them ran Raja, laughing, singing, and dancing. The sickly children reached for Raja but were unable to touch him. Raja continued to sing while the other children continued to cry. *How can there be such joy in the midst of all of this misery? There has to be a way that all people, especially all children, can find joy.*

Nic was only able to lean forward with assistance and sip the water that Raja offered him through his parched lips. He drifted in and out of consciousness, the same image of Raja and the children playing in his mind.

Three days had passed, the rays of the morning light shone through the small window on to Nic's bed. He opened his groggy eyes, trying to focus. Every inch of his body ached, especially his head. Slowly turning his head on his pillow, he saw people moving around him. For a moment he expected to see his mother and father, but the mosquito netting around his bed reminded him of where he was. Turning further to his left, he saw someone lying on the floor slightly below him, wrapped in a blanket. Nic tried to sit up and knocked a tin bowl of water off of his bed. The loud tin sound rolling on the cement floor startled Nic as he fell back. The body next to him on the floor rolled up in an instant.

"Nic!" Sabina yelled as she sprung up off of the floor.

Nic's head started to pound even more as his eyes focused on Sabina's excited face. "What's going on? Why were you on the floor?" Another body popped up from the floor. It was Raja.

Sabina started to laugh with tears rolling down her face. "You are all right?" she asked hopefully.

"Yes," Nic responded with surprise in his voice. "Yes. Of course I'm all right. I'm a bit hungry and achy, but why wouldn't I be all right?"

Sabina and Raja gleamed. “Carlos sent jars of peanut butter with flour and oil to make you flatbreads,” Sabina told him, “and a crate of chickens for the cook to prepare eggs for you. He even sent extra chickens to start a chicken coop here for the children.” Nic put his hands on his head and moaned.

“What, you do not like peanut butter and eggs?” asked Sabina, a bit upset.

“Yes, I do, but . . .,” Nic moaned. “My head hurts, and . . . .” Raja quickly held a bowl of water to his dry lips.

“Drink,” instructed Sabina. “You need strength. You have been very ill with malaria. I did not think you would live.”

“Not live?” Nic tried with force to sit up but only got onto one shaky elbow. “What do you mean?” he demanded weakly.

Sabina quickly helped him lay back down onto the bed. “You need to get strong. You must drink and eat. What shall I have the cook prepare for you? Some eggs or bread with peanut butter?”

Nic relaxed back onto his bed, breathing in deeply. “Rice, I’m hungry for rice.”

Sabina shook her head at her friend’s request for rice. “Once you are able to stomach the peanut butter and eggs, you will regain your strength quickly. The added protein will help you.”

The peanut butter and eggs remedy did help Nic recover and regain his strength as Sabina had predicted, but he still found it difficult to get through a day without resting periodically. He sat on the metal chair on his porch writing in his journal and reviewing the paperwork of the school. Nic looked up from his journal and pile of papers, taking a deep breath.

“I’m so glad I’m feeling better,” he sighed. He glanced around the campus at the groups of children studying quietly together. Nic rested his head back on the wall behind him and closed his eyes. His memories during his delirium were vague, except for the recurring vision of the children. *Where does Raja find his joy?* Nic questioned himself as the scene played in his head.

His deep thought was interrupted by chatter among the study groups across campus. One by one, each group of students started talking in uncharacteristically loud voices, looking around nervously. Curious, Nic closed his journal, never taking his eyes off the odd behavior of the students. One by one, the children began to stand and run in the same direction. Nic stood up quickly and ran after them. He caught up with two boys running hand-in-hand. One was quite young, and the older boy was patiently gauging his steps according to his companion's speed. "What's going on?" Nic asked in broken Hindi. He pointed towards the direction of the noise. The older boy began with his explanation, never taking his attention from the child holding his hand. Nic couldn't understand most of his explanation but could understand one word, bhaya—danger.

Nic ran faster, following the group to a building at the back of the compound. He could see a crowd gathering around something or someone near the welding workshop. Nic fought his way through the crowd. Breaking through, he found himself standing inside a large circle of people who were all staring at an opening in the ground. From deep below, he heard the faint sound of crying. Nic stepped up to the hole. It formed an awkward circle maybe five feet wide and was roughly lined with crumbling bricks. A boy had fallen into the abandoned well.

Nic looked down the deep hole, but there was nothing but darkness swallowing up the cries of a child. He scanned the crowd, hoping to see Uncle coming to the rescue, but he was nowhere to be seen. "Someone get a rope!" yelled Nic. Nobody moved. No one understood him.

Sabina suddenly broke into the clearing. She heard Nic's request while working her way through the crowd, and in Hindi, immediately repeated his call for rope. Two teenage boys retrieved a long thick rope from the welding workshop and quickly presented it to Nic. He grabbed it roughly and tied one end tightly around his waist. Throwing the other end of the rope to Sabina, he yelled, "Hold on!" as he got ready to climb down into the well. Sitting at the edge of the hole, he dangled his legs, waiting for the other end to be held securely.

Sabina grabbed the rope, commanding others to join her. A large number of boys picked up a section of the rope and wrapped it firmly around their arms, grasping it with their hands and bracing themselves. With a nod, Sabina ensured Nic that they were ready for his descent. Nic slid himself off the ground and into the hole. He was lowered into the well bit by bit as Sabina and the others loosened the rope with rushed jerks. As he was lowered deeper and deeper, the well became damper and darker. He focused on the cries of the child to gauge the location and status of the boy. The familiar voice sent fear through Nic. "Raja! Raja, is that you?" The cries became weaker. *I wonder how deep this thing is?*

Nic vowed not to panic as the rope continued to drop him down into the darkness. Suddenly, he was dropped into a pile of muddy rubbish. "No wonder the well dried up! It isn't deep enough," Nic mumbled in disbelief. "This hole can't be more than thirty feet deep."

Nic reached into the darkness. His touch located the boy, who groaned. "It's Raja!" He yelled up for the rope to be loosened, untied himself quickly, and helped Raja fasten it around himself. After making sure that the rope was secure, Nic directed his fellow rescuers to slowly pull him up. Nic released Raja, who was shaking with fright, as the rope began to tighten.

"Don't be afraid," Nic whispered. "You're safe."

Raja could not understand the words that Nic was saying but trusted the gentleness of his friend. He let go of Nic, grasping tightly to the rope. Nic felt him moving away as he was raised out of the hole. Moments later Nic could hear the cheers of the crowd as Raja reached safety. Nic knew it would take a few moments to untie the rope and return it down the hole, but the damp, smelly darkness was starting to get to him. He tried not to think about what he was standing in.

"Hey, don't forget about me," Nic yelled, trying to use a jovial tone of voice. The sudden brush of the rope on his face startled him. He laughed at himself as he tied the rope around his waist. He gave the rope a little tug and yelled up, prompting assent. As he rose up the well, he heard a faint whisper in his ear.

"Well done, Nic."

The voice didn't startle him as it was now a familiar one. For a moment, he thought he saw gold sparkles clinging to the walls of the well.

Raja's body was cut and bruised from his fall, and a deep gash in his left shin prevented him from walking. Nic carried him to a vacant room. The same doctor that tended to Nic wrapped Raja's wounded shin with layers of old yellowed gauze. "He must rest."

Nic didn't understand the doctor's words, but it was obvious that he wanted Nic to leave as he gently pushed him to the door. Nic caught Raja's eye and gave him a reassuring nod and smile. Raja returned the nod and smile. "Thank you," Raja said awkwardly, offering Nic the only two English words he knew.

Nic and Sabina stood barefoot on Nic's front porch, watching the rain. His time with Sabina and the children was coming to an end. "All this rain. It hasn't stopped raining for the last four weeks." Nic wiped beads of moisture from his forehead. "And I can't believe the humidity. It's ruined all of my TP."

Sabina laughed. "Good to see you have become accustomed to our ways out in the field."

Nic nodded. "Ah yes, the fields. Not much choice once the toilet broke down." Nic held the palm of his left hand under the rain. "It rains for three months straight here?"

Sabina nodded. She held her hand out into the dripping rain. "I'm afraid the rains will follow you to Calcutta when you go to work with Mother Teresa."

Nic didn't mind. He was looking forward to working with the legendary woman.

An old crippled woman who cooked for the hostel walked by carrying a large sack of rice. She was undaunted by the rain and flashed a smile to the pair staying dry under the porch. Nic sighed. "I've tried to carry that for her, but she won't let me."

Sabina offered her familiar giggle. "Yes, she is very stubborn and proud of her duty here."

Nic rubbed his chin. "You know, I don't think I have seen her yet without that big smile on her face."

"Yes, she is certainly very happy here."

"Why? Why is she so happy?"

Sabina called to the woman to join them on the porch. She quickly stepped through puddles and flopped the sack of rice on the dry porch. She was a small woman, dwarfed even more by her curved spine and hunched shoulders. Sabina bent down to her ear and asked her a question in Hindi. The cook stood as straight as her back would allow and with an even wider smile answered Sabina.

"She says she is happy because she has nothing, and she has everything."

Nic was perplexed. "I don't get it. How can she have nothing *and* everything?"

Sabina lowered her head. "I know a little of her story." She continued in a soft voice. "She came to us fifteen years ago, dying from the diseases leprosy had brought to her. Her family had thrown her away, literally, to the edge of their village, the same way most others here had been treated. She was alongside the road when I happened to pass by. I brought her here, and she responded very well to our simple treatments. She was cured but remained scarred and disabled for quite some time until she began to cook for us all. She is very grateful for her life being spared and praises God daily by working hard to feed the children here, her new family. The 'everything' that she has comes from being so spiritually rich and grateful for being led so close to God."

Nic smiled. "So she owns nothing, but has everything."

"Yes, indeed. Come, it is time for our visit to the elder camp," directed Sabina.

Nic smiled at the old woman and leaned over to lift the bag of rice for her. The woman gently placed her hand on Nic's and removed it from the bag. Nic let go of the bag with a smile. She gave Nic a nod and lifted the bag with a small grunt, splashing in a puddle of mud with her bare foot as she stepped out into the rain.

Nic and Sabina walked quickly through the hostel grounds to an area behind the children's school. The building at this location was small and had ten rooms inside where older lepers were being treated. A thin, elderly man approached them. He had snow-white hair and a meticulously trimmed beard. His teeth were few in his wide bright, smile. He extended his crippled hands to Nic, displaying many fingers that were shortened or missing. "God is Good, God is Good, Namaste."

Nic responded with a reverent bow. "Namaste."

The elder continued on his way, smiling and waving to all around him. "God is Good!"

"Every day the same joyful greeting," Sabina said, watching him. "He's another one that has nothing and everything. These people live on their faith of God and the joy of knowing that they are loved." She looked at the people around her. "They live in happiness because they are very close to God. Their lives are utterly simple. That allows them to be close to Him." She placed her hand on Nic's shoulder. "It has been good for you to be here with us, Nic."

"Yes, I have learned much. I can't believe our time together is drawing to a close."

Sabina's hand lowered to take Nic's. "Yes. Soon you will be leaving us. You have had many exciting times here." She started to chuckle. "My favorite is your new—what did you call it? Alarm clock."

"Thanks for reminding me. I'll never forget that morning when I reached for it. Somehow my hand snuck under the mosquito net above my head. I felt my fingers being pulled by the knuckles. When I woke up and looked up over my head, I saw two big red eyes. I jumped so high I knocked the netting over."

Sabina began to laugh uncontrollably. "And you broke it."

Nic shook his head. "That rat was as big as a lazy American cat."

Sabina looked at Nic's bandaged hand. "At least he only got the flesh on three of your knuckles."

"Yeah, great luck, huh?"

The lunch bell sounded from across the compound.

"Time for lunch," Nic said enthusiastically.

Sabina laughed. "No more problems with the rice?"

Nic joined in on the laughter. "No more problems. At first the thought of rice made me nauseous. Each night I dreamt of huge platters of food in a place back home. I just sat there, counting all the different flavors in a state of bliss. But after a few days the platters disappeared and I woke up hungry for the rice."

Sabina shook her head. "Your world is so different from ours. I don't think I could survive."

Nic smiled at his dear friend. "I'm going to visit Raja. Would you like to join me?"

"Yes, I would like that very much. I spoke with the doctor this morning, He says that he is healing slowly, but there is progress. I am praying that he will be able to walk soon."

Nic was happy to hear of Raja's progress and entered the room with a big smile on his face. His expression changed quickly when he saw the doctor and several staff members standing somberly next to Raja, who was lying motionless on a blanket on the floor. "What's happening?" Nic asked hesitantly.

Sabina relayed his question receiving the reply that she was afraid of. "Nic, Raja's wound has become infected, and the infection is quickly spreading through his body."

"Give him some antibiotics. That will stop the infection."

Sabina lowered her head. "We do not have any more medicine to give him. We receive very little. We rarely receive antibiotics."

Nic stepped closer to Raja. The gauze had been removed from his leg, revealing a deep, festering wound. "Why didn't they stitch the wound closed? This gauze isn't going to protect it from infection. Why didn't they do more for him?"

"Please understand, Nic. We do not have the supplies."

"But I brought medicine kits with me." Nic looked frantically around as if he was looking for the kits.

Sabina gently placed her hand on Nic's shoulder. "Yes, and we used them so quickly. There is nothing that we can do now."

Nic couldn't believe there was nothing that could be done. He spent the next three days sitting next to Raja, his head resting on Nic's lap, as his body slowly succumbed to the relentless infection. Nic felt so helpless.

"It was just a cut," he kept mumbling softly, wiping the tears from his eyes as he held his friend's limp hand.

Nic was shattered and devastated. He spent days walking the compound, trying to find peace in the loss of Raja. *You were my symbol of hope. You were joy among the misery. Maybe I was wrong. Maybe there isn't any hope for us.* "It was just a simple cut," he said to the clouds. "If only I brought more medicine. I want to help, but I couldn't even save this one sweet child." Nic reached to the sky, "If you want me to do this, you are going to have to send me help." A vision of Sara broke through the anguish of his mind. "I wish you were here," he said to the vision.

Nic sat on a large rock, looking out over the expansive rice field. He felt a hand lightly rest on his shoulder. He turned his head quickly. Michael stood regally next to him. "Oh, I was hoping you were . . ." Nic stopped.

"Sara," Michael finished for him.

"Yes, but that's impossible. Why would Sara be here?" Nic paused for a moment in thought. "Lately, it seems like she has been on my mind even more. In fact, I can even feel her." He stood up and began to walk slowly towards the field. Michael's hand continued to rest on Nic's shoulder as they walked side-by-side. "It was just a cut," blurted Nic, his frustration elevating his voice. "I felt so helpless. All I could do was hold his hand as he died. I couldn't help him." Nic stopped and looked at Michael. "I can't even help a little boy."

"What makes you think you didn't help him?"

"He died," answered Nic, his eyes tearing.

Michael placed both hands on Nic's shoulders. "The journey on earth will end for all humans, for the Creator has much more to share with you. That you cannot change. But what can be changed is the course of the journey."

Nic continued to look at Michael as he blinked away the tears. "I didn't change anything. Nothing changed."

Michael sighed. "Nic, close your eyes and think about Raja. What do you see?"

Nic closed his eyes. "I see him holding my hand, skipping next to me, smiling and laughing." Nic smiled at the memory of Raja's joy and then opened his eyes.

"Don't you understand, Nic? You cared."

"Caring isn't enough. Caring can't save anybody."

"Caring is the first step. You saw and experienced the joy of Raja. You loved him like a father would. It takes many steps to reach your destination."

Nic felt the touch of Michael's hands slowly release as his body faded. Nic found himself alone near the field. He turned to head back to the compound, not convinced that simply caring can really make a difference.

* * *

NIC'S FINAL FEW days at the hostel passed by quickly. He had mixed emotions about his departure. He could not shake the image of Raja's funeral pyre floating in a blaze of fire in the river. As he placed the last of his clothes in his bag, the scurry of the large lizard caught his eye. The lizard clung to the wall opposite him, its bulging eyes inspecting his activities as if it knew he was leaving and was disappointed that he wouldn't be there to bother anymore.

"You are one thing I won't miss." Nic closed his bag tightly. "Sorry, but I don't want any stowaways." Outside, Nic heard the laughter of the children. He loved to hear Raja laugh. Raja's joy created a laughter that was louder than any of the other children's.

He opened his door and stepped onto the simple porch. It was still raining lightly, but the children were enjoying the day as if the sun were shining. He rubbed his hand over the back of the old metal folding chair, recalling the many hours spent sitting on its hard seat writing in his journal and reviewing school papers with Raja by his side.

Sabina came from around the corner. "I have summoned a rickshaw. It will be here soon to take you to the train station. Do you have your things prepared to leave?"

Nic looked back through the open door. "Yes, I seem to have everything."

Sabina took Nic's hand. "It has been a blessing to have you with us. You have touched the hearts and lives of many. You will not be forgotten." With her other hand, she offered Nic a brightly colored batik of Jesus praying in a lotus position. "Some of the children made this for you to take on your travels. May God bless you and your work with His children."

"It's beautiful, thank you. I will keep it with me always." The pounding footsteps of the rickshaw driver echoed up the hill. "I guess this is my ride." The children saw the rickshaw and crowded around it. Nic gathered his bags and headed for his taxi.

"Uncle had to go into town today," Sabina said, "but asked me to extend his gratitude to you."

Nic nodded with a smile, "Please tell him the same from me." He rarely saw Uncle during his stay but enjoyed the brief moments when their paths crossed. Uncle always greeted Nic with a hug and a smile making him feel right at home.

Tossing his bags into the rickshaw, Nick turned to face the crowd that had gathered around him. He paused and looked around at the joyful faces around him: the proud cook, the happy old men, the doctor, the teens who got him the rope at the well, and the children—the smiling, happy children. In his mind's eye, Nic thought he saw Raja laughing with the joy he so easily felt. Nic took comfort in knowing that, even though he would never see these children again, Raja's enduring spirit would allow him to hold them in his heart forever.

Look at the joy on their faces, he thought. *They have so little, yet they live as if they have so much. There has to be something that can be done to make their lives easier. They deserve so much more.*

"God Bless you all!" Nic yelled. "Thank you!" He turned to Sabina. "Thank you so much for your help and friendship. It would have been a very difficult time without you."

Sabina bowed slightly. "It is you that I thank. I have enjoyed our time together. God bless you too."

Nic bowed toward Sabina and then reached out to her for a hug. They embraced, both doubtful they would ever see each other again.

Sabina then raised her hands in the air. The crowd quickly became quiet. "May God bless this traveler. May his journey be filled with peace as he travels on the road of Your will, oh Lord!" Sabina's commanding voice seemed to penetrate the heavens. The crowd began to chant a prayer of peace 'Om Ma Ni Pad Me Hum' wishing Nic joy.

Nic jumped onto the rickshaw and stood to wave to the adoring children. He sat down and took a deep breath, his eyes pooling with tears. Part of him wanted to jump off of the rickshaw and stay, but another part of him was anxious to continue his journey. Nic nodded to the driver who was waiting for his signal. The driver picked up the handles of the rickshaw and began to turn it around, heading down the hill. He noticed that this driver wasn't the same one that had brought him to the hostel. He was older and not as agile. He had difficulty straightening the rickshaw after making the turn, grunting and moaning as he fought with the contraption, trying to give his passenger the smoothest possible ride. It was yet another reminder to Nic of the many people that had difficulties and need help.

"It's time to move on. The spirit of hope never dies," Nic affirmed in his heart. The sound of the cheers became faint until they could finally no longer be heard. Nic held the batik to his chest. *I'll never forget you either,* he thought as he headed for the train station to begin his next adventure.

5

When you feel a peaceful joy,
that's when you are near the truth.
—Rumi

Nic arrived in Calcutta stepping onto the same treacherous platform but this time with much more confidence than when he first arrived. He cautiously took a deep breath, but the familiar smells of the depressed city burned his nose just like before. He had hoped that the recent rainfall might have washed away the foul odors, but it hadn't. Sandwiched among the crowd, he began to look for Carlos. Nic finally saw him struggling to make his way through the sea of bodies, trying to reach him. "Carlos!" yelled Nic with a high wave.

Carlos was unable to hear or see Nic in the commotion. The steady light rain didn't make the connection any easier. Nic began to jump up and down, bumping the travelers beside him. Although Nic was taller than most of the citizens, the number of noisy people and their chaotic movement made it difficult to focus on anything. "Carlos, over here!" Nic yelled even louder, trying once more to catch his attention.

Carlos noticed Nic's head and wave emerging from the crowd. He pointed to the edge of the platform behind Nic. Nic nodded and turned to work his way to freedom, breaking through the crowd to wait for Carlos, who finally emerged, tripping over a passenger's bag sitting on the ground. Nic caught his arm and helped him stand upright.

"Thanks," smiled Carlos.

"It's so good to see you," smiled Nic.

"Follow me, and stay close," instructed Carlos.

Nic was familiar with the routine. Their car was parked up the road. The crowd around the platform made it impossible to park any closer. Nic and Carlos got into their waiting transportation and headed for the place where Mother Teresa worked.

"It's good to see you so well," smiled Carlos. "You gave us quite a scare."

Nic shook his head, laughing to himself. "Thank you for the peanut butter and eggs. Once I could stomach them, they were the best medicine." Nic shifted in his seat, taking the batik gift from his pocket to show Carlos. "Their life is a simple and difficult one, but they are all so happy and appreciative."

"They are an amazing group of people, aren't they?" reflected Carlos.

"Yes," agreed Nic. He took the chance during the ride to the Mother House to tell Carlos more stories from his adventure in Bihar. The driver stopped in front of an alley sooner than he expected.

"We'll have other times to catch up," said Carlos. "Right now, it is time for you to start your next adventure." Carlos pointed to the tall, gated building. "Behind those gates is a world that you could never imagine. Your experiences at Bihar helped you grow. Your experiences here will feed your growth and stay with you forever." The building was tall and simple with one small door leading to an entry area. From there, they entered a big gate in a wall that surrounded the building. The tall cement wall was topped with jagged glass to deter nighttime intruders. The door was open from sunrise to sunset for anyone who needed help.

Mother Teresa knew through Carlos that Nic was arriving. She greeted him warmly but without fanfare. She felt that nobody was more important than another, including herself. She appeared very much as Nic had imagined, a very small and frail but gracious lady with weathered skin. But Nic would soon learn that, in spite of her physical frailty, there was a remarkable toughness and confidence about her. Nic noticed that her simple white-and-blue sari dragged in the dirt, covering her soiled feet. He could see that the many roads she had walked in her ministry showed painfully in her worn and scarred feet.

The female volunteers working with Mother Teresa numbered about forty. They also wore the traditional white-cotton sari trimmed with blue ribbon. Nic noticed that some of the volunteers wore simple flat sandals and others chose to always be barefoot.

"Bare feet remind me to stay humble," explained one of the workers.

Nic was assigned to assist the volunteers with their daily work. Many times a day, the bell at the gate was rung by a mother who willingly handed her newborn to the volunteers. Babies were also found abandoned at the gate, left in desperation by the parents who were unable to care for them. These distressed parents knew that Mother Teresa would feed, clothe, and teach their child much better than they could. It was the only way to offer a reasonable life to their offspring.

Nic enjoyed spending time in the large room filled with babies. Although there were five to seven infants in each crib, it was often a challenge to find space for a new child to rest comfortably. Nevertheless, room was always found. No baby was ever turned away.

"They are just like the baby I found in the street," said Nic, sharing his horrifying experience with a volunteer. As much as the tiny faces of the innocent babies pulled on his heartstrings, nothing compared to the agonizing faces of the lonely people dying on the streets just outside. Mother Teresa did not want anyone to leave this world without knowing that somebody cared. She did not want these unfortunate people to die alone. Nic was told that Mother once held a dying woman in her arms for six hours. When she was told she missed very important meetings that day and that important decisions were not made because of her absence, Mother explained, "I had something much more important to do." The woman was afraid of dying alone, and Mother had assured her she would not. Mother kept her word.

Nic only found a few precious opportunities to work closely with Mother Teresa during his four-week stay. He was thrilled when he had the opportunity on his last day to join Mother Teresa and Beth, a young doctor from Boston, in a makeshift examination room set up near the front door of the house. Mother chose this location to shorten the distance someone would need to be carried in from the street. Nic knew that Mother was aware his days at the house were coming to an end and was flattered that she chose to spend much of that day working with him. Mother passed the towel to Nic.

"Come help to bring in this man. The workers have just found him near the train station. He is in much pain."

Nic stepped outside and returned with two assistants as they carried an old dying man on a stretcher. They gently laid him down on a high table. Mother promptly began to wash his skin with a sponge and warm water she had prepared. The old man began crying loudly. Nic stood back silently. His heart hurt for the old man.

"Mother, ask him if he will take an injection of morphine to kill the pain so you can finish washing him for the exam," said Dr. Beth.

Mother turned and gently asked him. As the old man replied to her, his face began to light up and his crying subsided. He reached out and brushed his shaking hand gently across Mother's cheek as he responded. Mother continued washing the man. "He says he is not crying of pain as he is numb and feels nothing because of the leprosy."

"Then why is he weeping?" asked Nic.

Mother never hesitated in her washing of the man. "He says this is the first time anyone has touched him since he was a child."

Dr. Beth approached the man, stroking his dirty hair. "I guess that may be fifty or so years."

"He looks so much older," observed Nic.

Mother laughed. "We all do here. Sometimes, there isn't much for the body to live on."

Her response reminded Nic of something he had been wanting to ask her. He seized the opportunity. "They tell me that you haven't taken a solid meal in years. You only eat scraps that are left at the end of the day after the others are fed. How can you keep going all day only to eat the little that is left at the end of the day?"

Mother smiled as she finished wiping down the man. "The hungry must be fed first. I eat little because I have no hunger for earthly food. My nourishment comes from God. The only meal that matters is the daily joy of caring for others. It is all that this old body and soul needs."

"I'll take it from here. You two can go now," interrupted Dr. Beth. "I know you're leaving soon, Nic, and you'll want some time with Mother. Good luck on your travels."

Mother handed Dr. Beth the sponge. Drying her hands on a small towel she turned to Nic.

"Nic, come walk with me," she said solemnly.

Nic was happy to have the time alone with Mother. They walked in silence for a few moments. "There is so much poverty here," said Nic, breaking the silence. "Even the Lord said we will always have our poor and . . ."

Mother interrupted. "He said exactly that. There will always be the poor as long as there is greed and injustice, but he never said the poor had to suffer so unnecessarily. That's where we come in, Nic, people like you, me, and our volunteers who share what they have to help make someone else's life a little better. There is much poverty everywhere in the world. But none of it is like what I have seen in places of extreme wealth."

They reached the top of the steps and sat side-by-side on a wooden bench in the hall. Nic turned to her. "Poverty in wealthy nations?"

Mother nodded. "In the USA, especially."

"I know we have poverty, but I have never heard of poverty in our country that is worse than what you have right here."

Mother looked at him deeply. "I have visited your country many times. Did you know, Nic, that there is leprosy there too?"

Nic shook his head. He had never seen or heard of human suffering in the States like the suffering he had seen in India.

"But I have seen things worse than leprosy there," said Mother with concern.

"Mother, tell me, what could be worse than what I have seen here?" Nic was almost afraid to hear the answer.

"Once I visited a nursing home for the elderly. There was a beautiful old woman who sat there every day, just staring at the front door. She was waiting for her son to visit. He never did, they said. That's a form of poverty far more severe than Calcutta's slums."

Nic sat up straight. "Surely you speak of a different kind of poverty?"

Mother shook her head. "Poverty does not exist here as you think. Last week, I delivered food to a Muslim mother of five hungry children. She was full of tearful gratitude as she told me to wait, that she would return quickly. I watched her divide the rice I brought her into two piles. She gathered one pile, smiled at me and said, 'Today I am a wealthy woman,' and walked out the door. I watched her as she shared the rice with the Hindu woman next door. Tell me, in what you have seen here, are the people you call poor truly sad? Or, does the sadness come from within when you realize that having physical things does not make you happy?"

Mother paused a moment, receiving a silent answer from Nic through his eyes. "You accumulate more, yet you feel empty," she continued. "Poverty is being without the necessities to live. But there is no life without the love of God. Everything else is empty stuff. And do you not find that you are rarely grateful for it? Yes, yes, I fear that poverty comes from within."

Nic nodded with his thoughts far away. They sat together for a moment in a heavy silence.

Mother broke the silence and started to chuckle, pointing to Nic's shirt. It read "Happiness is . . . a cold beer." Mother nudged Nic with her sharp elbow, smiling. "Do you believe that is true?"

Nic looked down, feeling a bit ridiculous. "Yes Mother, right now, in this heat, a cold beer would make me very happy."

Mother laughed. Nic loved to hear Mother Teresa laugh. Her giggles were light and genuine like those of a little girl. Her spirit seemed to recharge with each chuckle. Nic absorbed as much of her spirit as he could receive.

A worker approached them. She was unaware of the content of their conversation but smiled and chuckled with their contagious laughter. She handed Mother a note. Mother's face returned to reality and she looked at Nic. "Carlos advises he cannot take you to the airport. I will send someone with you."

Nic put up his hands, still energized from their short time of sharing. "No need, but thank you. I will find my way without a problem. Your work here is far more important to attend to."

Mother nodded and gave Nic a frail but firm hug. "Very well. I will not be here in the morning when you leave, so I will now say my goodbye. God bless you and thank you for your help. Go and keep serving. And, oh yes, don't forget to say goodbye to the babies."

Nic stood beside her. Her small stature barely reached his shoulders. They walked down the hall to a simple prayer room. Mother bowed reverently as she entered the room. Moving to the center of the large empty room, she bowed again and sat on the hard floor in prayer. Nic noticed how tiny her frail seated presence was in the large rectangular room.

Bowing, Nic left her there in prayer, then turned to go further down the hallway and entered the nursery where numerous workers were tending to the needs of at least fifty large bassinets. Some babies were coughing, but few were crying.

They have nothing yet they have everything because of their spirit of generosity and hope. Goodbye little ones. Grow strong! Nic blew a kiss in the air, praying that a bit of his blessing reached each innocent child there. He stepped outside into the street and looked around. A group of children ran by. The tiniest of the group bumped into Nic, giggling. She was small with her dark long hair hanging in her eyes. Nic noticed her wrapped up arm. He seemed to recognize the face, the hair, the giggle. Nic held her to keep her from falling. "You look like my friend Sara." He leaned over to look into her face. "Let me see your arm. Are you okay?"

The little girl abruptly backed up, frightened, and ran away from Nic. Nic straightened up and watched her run to catch up with the others. *I wonder how Sara is. I wonder if I will ever find out.*

* * *

NIC ARRIVED IN Dandora just outside of Nairobi, Kenya in East Africa. Kenya was to be the next leg of his service mission.

Jambo! There was something about this word often used by the locals that made Nic feel like celebrating. The weather was dryer and cooler in Dandora than in India, especially at night, and a greater variety of food was available.

Nic had been looking forward to his time with this volunteer charitable group. They had operated in the region for decades opening and running clinics and building schools, churches, and communities. Most were from America, and many of them were even acquaintances of Nic's from his seminary days. Many of the other volunteers were African, which added to the diversity and success of the group.

Nic soon made a special new friend named Tommy, a laid-back guy who looked like he had just stepped out of the sixties. His soft sandals, baggy shirt, and shaggy beard showed off his comfortable style. But despite his down-to-earth, relaxed demeanor, Tommy was the brilliant mastermind behind many of the program's accomplishments. The people of Dandora had grown to love Tommy as much as Nic soon would.

The group was in charge of a special development, the first of its kind, that was conceived and funded by the World Bank and United Nations. It was to become a planned network of communities with concrete slabs, running water, and sewage systems that would be located near the Mathari Valley. This area had come to be known as the world's largest slum. It had no running water, no sewage, and only mud homes. Over 250,000 people made their home in this slum. The many residents of the valley were entered into a raffle and given a chance to leave. If their name was drawn, the winner got a slab in the Dandora development to build their house upon. They then spent their days in a nearby volcanic quarry chiseling out the sand and aggregate needed to create and pour concrete blocks. These blocks were transported back to their home site and used for the construction of the walls.

Nic stayed in a simple home shared by the volunteers and their guests. The front door of the house was a simple gate that opened to an airy, cement courtyard. The wide cement hallways led to six bedrooms, a kitchen, a small gathering room, and the chapel. These rooms were under a roof, while the open courtyard was used as a gathering area for meetings, meals, and relaxation. The house and the ground blended together into a sea of grey cement. It was dull, but it had a welcome sterile feeling in contrast to the filth of the slums nearby.

Nic did not arrive in Dandora to the fanfare that he received when he arrived in Bihar; there were no crowds, no cheers, no celebration. He was actually a bit disappointed to be put to work within the first half hour of his arrival. He barely got settled into his room when a trowel was placed in his hand.

The volunteers had been busy building a community center in the middle of the development next to a church when Nic arrived. "I want to do more than spread cement on bricks," mumbled Nic as he helped smooth out the globs of cement between each volcanic brick. He looked around and noticed that every building in the complex looked pretty much the same. He had never seen so much grey cement. Even the concrete bricks from the volcano quarry were grayish in color. There wasn't foliage of any kind within the cement city. At least the complex in Bihar had trees and bushes to liven up the place.

Nic was finally asked to begin the work he had requested to do: supply and distribute medicine to the neighboring tribes. Now he felt like he could make a difference. He expected a long instruction session with Tommy regarding the details and dangers of his journey. Instead, he was handed a sheet of paper with directions, a compass, camping gear, food, water, and supplies for the tribes. The only strong advice that Tommy gave Nic was "Do not offend the members of the tribes."

"Is there anything else I should know?" questioned Nic.

Tommy shrugged his shoulders. "You'll learn as you go. Just follow your directions and pay attention to your surroundings. You'll be fine."

The directions were difficult for Nic to follow, consisting only of the number of kilometers that he should travel in a certain direction. There weren't any roads to take when traveling across the Kenyan plains. Even though this country belonged to the millions of animals that called it home, the vast plateau was mesmerizing and it sometimes seemed empty because of its grand size. Nic stopped his jeep and looked around. He felt like he was going around in circles and getting nowhere.

"I'm sure I followed these directions perfectly," grumbled Nic, holding the paper up in one hand and the compass in the other. He studied the directions, reviewing the path he took in his head. "These directions must be wrong." He lowered his arms with a huff and looked around. The flat land seemed to never end as it wrapped around the horizon. Nic reached for the black radio transmitter on the seat beside him. "I hope this thing works," he said as he flipped the power switch. The old box hummed briefly as a green light flickered. Nic held the transmitter close to his mouth. The green light turned black and the box stopped humming before he could begin his plea for help. He flipped the switch again and again with no success. "What am I supposed to do now?" Nic threw down the transmitter, banging his fist on the box. "Which way do I go?" he yelled to the blank landscape around him.

"Follow your heart." The voice startled Nic.

"Why do you do that?" barked Nic. Michael stood next to the jeep. "Why do you keep sneaking up on me like that?"

"How can I sneak up on you when I am always here?" Nic was not in the mood for Michael's puzzling comments.

"Are you here to help me find my way?" hoped Nic, holding the piece of paper in front of Michael's face.

"You won't find your way on the paper, Nic. The way to go is inside of you."

Nic scowled. "I never know what you are talking about." Nic slumped back in his seat.

"Nic, you look for guidance in the wrong places. You look outside of yourself. Look within and you will find direction."

Michael walked to the front of the jeep and looked at the vast open land ahead. "The Maasai tribe that you seek are a happy people full of tradition and celebration. They do not depend on the outside world to direct them. They depend on each other and the traditions passed down through many generations. They look inside themselves."

"But I don't know how to get to them." Nic got out of the jeep and stood next to Michael. "I need directions."

"The spirit inside of you will direct you. Be still and listen." Michael walked to the side of the jeep, leaving Nic standing alone.

"My spirit? How does my spirit know where to go?" Nic turned towards Michael. "He's gone again," muttered Nic as he hung his head.

He stood alone, looking around. With a sigh, he closed his eyes, standing totally still. His eyes sprung open. "I think I know which way to go," whispered Nic with surprise.

He got in the jeep, glanced at his directions and held up the compass. "It's this way," he told himself confidently, proud of his accomplishment. "I guess I just got upset and couldn't think clearly."

"Everybody is always so happy," pondered Nic when he arrived at the Maasai village. His arrival sparked a celebration. Nic was greeted with a gourd that had a hole in the top of the stem. Hoping for a drink of water after his long nerve-wracking journey, he held the hole to his mouth and tipped the gourd. He was surprised to feel a warm liquid enter his mouth which tasted like warm milk mixed with dirt. While ingesting the strange drink, Tommy's parting words—"Do not offend the members of the tribes"—echoed in his head. He swallowed, trying not to think about what he might have just put into his body. He later found out that the gourd was filled with the traditional celebration drink: warm cow's milk mixed with blood from a bull.

The welcome continued with their traditional celebration dance. The Maasai men stood straight, bent their knees slightly, and then sprung up into the air. Each time they landed, they sprung off the ground harder and rose into the air higher and higher. As they reached their maximum height, they tucked their legs up under their body and created a space of at least four feet between themselves and the ground, chanting continuously.

"If the NBA could only see these guys." Nic tried many times to jump like the Maasai, but his average stature only ended up creating more of an awkward comedy show than a show of celebration.

Dispersed between the Maasai villages were the Kikuyu people, hardworking agriculturalists who grew crops and raised small animals. In contrast to the Maasai, who were tall and thin, the Kikuyu were short and round. The Kikuyu celebrated Nic's arrival with a special meal of boiled hippopotamus skin. Nic was unable to even bite off a piece of their delicacy. The Kikuyu put the entire piece in their mouth and chewed it into a ball that they keep in their cheek to be chewed on throughout the day, slowly absorbing the fat obtained from the tough skin.

The joy that the people shared with Nic, and with each other, made him feel like he was in another world. "These people have so little, but they always have so much to celebrate," Nic shared with his colleagues upon his return. "If only everybody would honor each other and depend on each other as they do. If we all worked together, every day would be a celebration for all of us."

6

There are those who give with joy,
and that joy is their reward.
—Khalil Gibran

A large firewood-lined hole burned while Nic and the volunteers spent the entire morning preparing food for the Christmas Eve celebration at the compound. When the fire burned out, the hot coals that remained in the open-air oven were covered with fresh green palm branches. The food for their celebration—in this case chickens, potatoes, and vegetables—was elaborately placed on these branches and then covered with fresh greens. It slowly cooked for the next few hours to perfection.

Tommy and Nic relaxed on wooden chairs in the courtyard, resting from the morning's lengthy chore.

"So, Nic," said Tommy, "this is your first Christmas away from home?"

Nic smiled like a little boy spending his first summer away at camp. "Yes. Can you tell? Is it that obvious?"

Tommy laughed. "Actually, your parents wrote me, asking me to make sure you get a package they sent. It just arrived yesterday." He retrieved the package from the house. A bit battered on the corners and edges, it must have had quite an adventurous trip from Pennsylvania to Dandora.

Nic quickly opened it. He was ecstatic. "I was hoping they wouldn't forget!" He held up a large red suit.

"They write you've been St. Nick for quite some time."

Nic chuckled. "This will be the seventh year."

"Seven years? What makes you do it every year?"

Nic lowered the suit, remembering his first time as Santa Claus. "It began when I was in high school. I organized the school's first toy drive."

They were on break with no more duties, so Tommy listened as Nic reminisced, telling the story of how he organized ten of his classmates to help out on the drive. He sketched out the scene of the students scrambling around the high school cafeteria methodically filling cardboard boxes with toys for delivery to needy children. Each box was clearly labeled with its destination address, and inside were neatly wrapped gifts marked with the appropriate gender and age. Nic explained to Tommy how he had recruited willing "elves" to help him with the project. He had been very pleased with the response from so many of his schoolmates, who had collected more toys than they had hoped for.

Nic felt himself merge with the story, still so vivid within him from high school as he continued to narrate to Tommy . . .

A boy had walked into the cafeteria dressed in baggy clothes. A large-lens camera hung around his neck. He was a member of the school yearbook staff. "Wow! It looks like Santa's workshop in here." The group grinned with pride. "Would you all mind taking a short break and getting together for a picture? We need to get a shot of the school's first-ever toy drive for the yearbook."

Nic's band of elves left their stations and gathered in front of the wrapping table to pose for a yearbook picture. Four sloppy Santas were in the bunch.

"Okay now, everyone say . . . Merry Christmas." instructed the photographer.

The gang of friends all yelled, "MERRY CHRISTMAS!"

After the photo was taken, the helpers went right back to work, filling up the last box of gifts. It was taken to a big station wagon, barely fitting into the wagon's storage section that was already loaded with other boxes. Nic clapped his hands, calling the crowd to attention. "Okay, cars are packed, and everyone has their route and drivers. Remember, fellow helpers and Santas, be *merry*." Everyone climbed into their "sleighs." Just before they took off, Nic leaned out the window, holding on to his wig and hat. "All together now."

"Ho ho ho!" everyone cheered as they pulled out of the school parking lot heading off in different directions.

Nic was crunched into the back seat of his "sleigh." He reached over and lightly tapped the driver. "Hey, Chelsea, you're in charge of the reindeer. Do you know where to lead them?"

"Yes I do, Santa. Our first stop is coming up. I think this is Beacon Street." Chelsea strained to check the approaching street sign and, confirming the street, made a sharp right turn. She drove slowly, looking at each house for a number. The expression on her face gave away what she was thinking. *I can't believe people live like this*. It was like they had entered a black-and-white world. The houses were dull and colorless. Every home was in need of some sort of repair. She spotted a porch awning propped up by a warped plank of wood, lots of houses with broken windows replaced with plastic, and holes in some of the roofs that were covered with black tarps. She slowly passed a house whose screen door hung loosely on its hinges opening to a yard cluttered with forgotten potted plants. An uneasy feeling raced through Chelsea as she arrived at their destination. "This is it, Santa."

Nic got out of the car and opened the trunk. He placed the appropriate gifts into a large soft red velvet bag. Chelsea stayed in the car feeling a bit stunned, looking at her surroundings. "Come on, Chelsea, Santa needs his helper." He grabbed hold of the bag and slung it over his shoulder. Chelsea quietly got out of the car and joined Nic. She closed the trunk, and they walked up to the first door.

Nic turned to Chelsea. Their eyes met with the same expression. The front door seemed ready to fall off of its hinges. They could smell an odor of damp rotten wood. "Better try the doorbell," suggested Nic. "This door may fall apart if we knock on it."

Chelsea agreed. She was dressed like an elf, and she tried her best to put on her biggest smile. "Here we go." She reached for the doorbell.

The bell rang, and immediately there was screaming inside. The door burst open and three little girls ran out on to the porch yelling "Santa! Santa! Santa's here, Mommy!"

The oldest took Nic's hand and led him inside to their tiny kitchen. Nic knew from the family's wish list that this girl was seven years old and that her sisters were just a few years younger. Chelsea followed, wrinkling her nose at the pungent odor of soiled dishes and smoke. A woman sat at the table staring blankly, cigarette in hand, drinking gin from a water glass.

"Hello, Santa. Merry Christmas." The woman raised her glass in the air toward Nic and brought the glass to her lips.

The children's dirty faces looked up at Nic, eyes beaming. Their joy and innocence touched him deeply. Chelsea glanced around the cluttered room, eyeing the sink of dirty dishes that caused the distinct odor.

Nic felt a firm yet gentle tug. The smallest sibling held Nic's robe firmly in her hand. "Santa, I know I haven't always been good, but did you maybe bring me something? It doesn't have to be much."

"Of course I brought you something. I brought something for all of you." Nic smiled at the children and motioned to Chelsea to open the bag. They both began handing out the gifts to the excited children. Chelsea blinked away the tears that welled up in her eyes and reached into the bag.

The mother got up, opened the door to a sparse refrigerator, and grabbed a bottle of gin. She scowled with disgust. "Good thing you're here, Santa. I don't have any money to buy them nothing."

Suddenly there was a shriek just outside the front door. "It's Santa! He's *here*! I told you I saw him."

"I think we need to get going, Santa."

"Sounds like you're right," agreed Nic as he reassembled his sagging belly. "We have many more stops to make."

Nic and Chelsea wished a cheery "Merry Christmas" to the unfortunate family and stepped outside. A small group of giddy children was skipping toward them. Nic would have loved to stop and hug each one of the smiling barefoot children, but he had to settle for a quick tussle of his fingers through their messy hair as he walked by. Chelsea and Nic got inside the car. Nic waved goodbye as they slowly pulled away in silence.

After a few moments, Chelsea broke the heavy silence. "Wow."

"It's unpleasant to see how some people live, isn't it?"

"I wanted to get out of there as quickly as possible, but I didn't want to leave the children," Chelsea shared as they approached the next house. It was badly in need of repair. Deteriorating shingles on the roof surrounded a large black tarp that loosely covered a gaping hole as it flapped in the wind. The gift bearers stepped carefully up the front walk, dodging the rusty bikes, worn tires, and broken glass that littered the entranceway. Armed with a bag full of toys, they tapped on the door. A tired voice invited them to come in. Nic and Chelsea opened the door and cautiously walked into the living room. There they saw five listless, hungry-looking children sitting around a television. The two oldest were eight-year-old twin boys. The others were three girls sitting closely together, ages three, five, and six. Slouched on the couch behind them were four adults, drinking beer and smoking. The coffee table was piled with leftover chips and candy bars. Empty beer bottles crowded a dining table laden with overflowing ashtrays.

"Look who's here kids, it's Santa," said one of the men between gulps of his beer. He winked hard at Nic.

The children turned and their faces lit up. But they didn't run to Nic like the children in the last house. They each glanced at the adults as if they were afraid that a response would get them in trouble.

"Here, Santa," Chelsea said, handing Nic the bag of gifts. "Give them these."

Nic reached his hand into the bag but found himself glancing at the adults for permission, just like the children.

"Santa brought ya'll something, kids." A disheveled man stood up and walked to the kitchen, yawning loudly. The children watched as the refrigerator door opened. Their faces dropped as it was closed.

Nic made a noble attempt at a full belly "Ho Ho Ho!" with little response from the room full of people. "There you go. Go ahead, open them. Merry Christmas." The youngest took her gift and turned it over, inspecting the wrapped package.

"Look out everyone. We're out of cans. Somebody's turn to make a run after these." The man returned to the couch with a lazy thud, slamming the six-pack on the table.

The little girl held the package and looked at one of the women.

"Go ahead, honey."

The girl tore open the wrap to reveal a Raggedy Ann doll. She held it up to show it to the woman.

"That is a Christmas gift from all of us, honey. Give it a hug."

The girl gently held the doll up in front of her, looking deep into its face. She let go of the doll with her right hand and began to trace its curvy stitched smile with her finger. She then held the doll tight against herself and continued to watch the television. Each child opened their gift and returned to their lazy stupor.

Santa and his elf weren't sure what to do. The children's lack of energy was disturbing. Nic turned to Chelsea. "Come on, elf. Time to go."

"Why the rush?" Chelsea asked as they got into the car.

Nic stared forward and sighed. "They need food and medicine and clothes, not toys. Next stop, the grocery store."

Nic paused, realizing he had gotten lost in his own story. "We couldn't believe people lived like that. It actually made me angry."

Tommy nodded. He totally understood Nic's frustration.

"My mother made this for me," said Nic, holding up the suit. "Ever since I can remember, I've wanted to be St. Nick and spread the spirit of sharing." He realized that others had joined them while he was telling his story. "Do the locals here know about Santa Claus?"

Tommy looked for an answer at the others who had joined them to admire Nic's gift. He got little response. "I'm not too sure, but I know the perfect time for you to wear it. Let's have Santa show up this afternoon at the center where we do weekly food and medicine distribution." The others laughed, agreeing that it would be quite a sight to see Santa at the distribution.

"Well then, I better get myself ready," said Nic, rising to his feet. "Ho ho ho!" he chanted as he entered the house. He went to his room, closed the door, and hugged the Santa suit like a child cuddling a favorite teddy bear. "Thanks Mamma," he whispered. "And Merry Christmas to you too."

That afternoon, a group of volunteers was busy registering families for food pickup. Others were signing up for classes being offered. The long line consisted of mostly women and children. Marya, one of the local teens, entertained the children while standing in line by telling them the story of St. Nick. She hadn't heard of the jolly 'ole elf until the night before, but she eagerly volunteered to share the story that she had become enthralled with. Nic couldn't understand Marya, but Tommy assured Nic that she had captured the true spirit of the story. Nic noticed Marya had long dark hair, and her eyes danced as she seemed to speak without even taking a breath. *Sara's voice would have the same enthusiasm and her eyes the same sparkle*, thought Nic as he pictured his rendition of Sara telling the same story.

The children started to crowd around, grabbing at Nic and yelling excitedly in Kiswahili. Nic had a hard time keeping the beard and wig on as the children jumped on him, grabbing at the white fluff. "Easy there kids, slow down."

Marya recognized Nic's predicament. She turned to the children and yelled in Kiswahili, "*Tamari*! *Tayari*! *Simama*!" They stopped suddenly and stood attentively.

Tommy approached as Nic was straightening his Santa hat. Nic was looking a bit flustered. "Everything okay here Nic?"

"Thanks to Santa's helper, all seems to be all right now. I don't know what she said, but whatever it was, it worked."

Tommy laughed. "I think they are excited because they've just learned that Santa will give them the gifts they really want."

"What does it mean when they say *baba*?"

Finding Hope in Rocky Waters

Shadoe Stevens

Opening Friday, December 6th

6:30 PM

Stakenborg Greenberg Fine Art

1545 Main St Sarasota

941-487-8001

Transcendental Wha Hoo

Amid the incandescent colors
lubricating and elevating awareness,
a revelation comes with a whammy
A world of cities and temples and monasteries
an entire universe is contained in a mystical diagram
With a yawn, geometric shapes,
containing all of creation, reveal a passage
into a visable and mysterious
3rd dimension with a 2 dimensional space
a gateway into the storehouse of good fortune.
Miracles, flowing with milk and honey,
transform all those who gaze within,
guiding and awakening our highest ideals.
It is a three dimensional blueprint
a good luck charm oozing with magical power.

Tommy shook his head sadly. "It means they want their daddies."

Nic looked at the children. Blinking away his tears, he turned back to Tommy. "Where are their fathers?"

"Gone. They are gone because of war, work, or death. Many suffer from debilitating disease. There is a growing health concern here because too many men are dying, even at a young age. And now we are starting to see women and children with the same symptoms. I am sorry to say that our usual medicines aren't working. It's like their entire immune system shuts down in a rapid period of time."

Nic kept looking around at the crowd of children. "Why do these people have so many children? Especially when they know they will have to suffer? I just don't get it."

Tommy nodded. "It's a hard thing to explain. I used to think it was because so few survived. I've come to realize it's far more complex."

"Tell me. I want to understand." The Santa suit was hot and uncomfortable. Nic ignored the beads of sweat that were rolling down his forehead and stinging his eyes as he waited for the answer.

Tommy paused to gather his thoughts. Then he began. "Well, in the States, we're very busy with the many demands and responsibilities of our daily lives. We are occupied with work, families, schools, clubs, and the like. Our lives may be complicated, but we have a lot of control over them. We have virtually endless options to choose from and enjoy. Here, virtually none of those opportunities exist. These people have to spend their days just trying to stay alive. They have to scramble to secure their food for the next day or to obtain the firewood and medicines that are also critical for their survival. That's it for most of them."

"But I still don't understand why they continue to have so many children. If they were to stop having children, there would be fewer mouths to feed."

"These people have no control over their lives. They have very few possessions and very little joy, except for one thing. Having children is the only thing that they can control and possess that gives them joy. A child is so much more to them than just another mouth to feed."

Nic finally understood. "So, having a child gives them a sense of control over their lives. It gives them purpose. Without children, they would feel like they were just existing from day to day and would have nothing to call their very own."

Tommy nodded.

"And much of the Third World is like this?" Nic asked.

"Yes, and sadly, most of the world *is* Third World." Tommy read the despair on Nic's face. "Every child gives them hope for tomorrow. Their daily lives may be painful, but their children are there to compensate by providing them with a great deal of joy."

Nic thought about Raja and the children in Bihar, the joy on their faces and their spirit of hope.

Tommy placed his hand firmly on Nic's shoulder. "We come here to widen their options for a meaningful life. We help alleviate some of the pain while we offer them a lot of hope that this life is not in vain."

Nic's attention went back to the children. "I need to spend some time with the kids for a bit of fun before I change out of this suit." He looked past the people receiving sugar, flour, vegetable oil, and medicines and saw a group of people sitting on the ground, rubbing the oil that they received on their heels and feet. He turned back to Tommy, pointing to the group. "What are they doing that for? Isn't the oil needed for cooking?"

"The air and earth are so dry here that the skin on their feet is cracking. The oil soothes the pain. Fortunately, they have water to cook with here."

Nic shook his head as he slowly headed for the kids. "Everything is so different," he said to himself. "How can so many people all live so differently in the same world? How can they all be helped?"

That evening, a crowd gathered outside for the Christmas Eve celebration, the first in their new open-air community center. Nic noticed that the sky above the center was a brilliant blanket of stars and that there was a certain quiet and stillness in the air. An unexpected breeze began to blow in dark and heavy clouds that gathered quickly, blotting out the stars. Few noticed the impending weather, caught up in the peace and love of the celebration as they sang songs of worship.

A sudden downpour startled the gathering. Nic instinctively turned to run for cover, expecting the rest of the crowd to do the same. But instead of running for cover from the hard rainfall, the crowd stayed in their places, singing loudly and raising their hands to the sky. "He reigns, He reigns!" praised the ecstatic crowd, singing at the top of their lungs to the heavens. Children splashed and played in the growing puddles. Laughter and singing spread through them like wildfire as the rain beat down harder and harder. Nic stood still, a bit stunned by the reaction, being bumped around by the dancing crowd as they slowly began to disperse, still bellowing in loud song.

Nic and his friends finally ran to the house, laughing and dodging big puddles along the way. They entered the gate, splashing with each step as they headed across the courtyard and down the hall to the gathering room for shelter. Walking through the door dripping, they were each handed a small towel to dry off the best they could. The crowd's enthusiasm was contagious. "That was really something, these people are alive!"

Tommy rubbed his head with a towel. "With five years of drought, and this being the middle of the dry season, this is quite a Christmas blessing from heaven. Let's celebrate with this." Reaching into a cabinet, Tommy took out a bottle and began to pour a small amount of its contents into short, round glasses.

Nic held up the glass of clear liquid, swirling it around gently. "What is it?"

Tommy raised his glass. "A local brew called *Changaa*. It's like moonshine here. Merry Christmas!" He brought the glass to his lips and emptied it in one gulp.

Nic waved the glass under his nose. "Smells like kerosene. Can you run your car on this stuff?" With his eyes closed, Nic downed the shot. He grimaced, his body reacting to the drink with a shiver.

Tommy cheered. "Knew you could do it. Have some more."

Nic hesitated, then held out his glass for a refill as did others who entered the room. "There is a lot for us to be thankful for, a lot to celebrate, isn't there?" remarked Nic, bracing himself for another round.

"Yes, my boy, there certainly is," agreed Tommy, and together they emptied their glasses with a hard gulp.

One by one, the other guests succumbed to the soothing effects of the *Changaa* and retired to their rooms. Only Tommy, Nic, and three other guests remained in the sitting room. After one more glass of *Changaa*, Nic wished a good night to all, picked up his lantern, and headed for his bedroom. His room was at the far end of the house. The only other room at that end was another bedroom that belonged to a guest named Bill. Outside the door to his room, Nic hung up his extinguished lantern on a hook and closed the door behind him. He slipped off his wet sandals and set them on the window ledge to dry. The window was small and void of any glass or screen and opened to the back of the building. Nic collapsed onto his bed and, with the help of the soothing *Changaa*, fell right to sleep.

Nic was awakened by a loud fluttering around his head. He jumped up out of bed, startled. Using his pillow, he tried to swat a large bug flying aimlessly around his room. It was the size and thickness of his index finger with wings that were each three inches long. "If I can handle a big lizard in my room, I can certainly take care of one big bug," he chuckled to himself as he awkwardly swung his thin pillow through the air. He finally struck a fatal blow to the bug, and it fell to the floor with a thud. Satisfied with his victory, he started to get back into bed, but before he could lie down, he was disturbed to see a few more of the same kind of bug beginning to fly into his room through the open window. He pulled his mattress off the bed and covered the window with it, sealing the intruders' only entrance. Swatting the bugs with a towel, Nic concentrated on his enemies, striking them one by one. He was finally satisfied that he had defeated the intruders.

Curiosity led him to open his door and look for the source of the attack. Nic opened his door to a moving shadow of a massive swarm. He couldn't believe his eyes. Thousands of bugs were swarming outside. Panicking, he slammed the door closed, peering through the keyhole. He could barely make out the white wall on the other side of the sidewalk that was only ten feet away because of the thickness of the swarm. With a few swats from his towel, he again cleared his room of any flying menaces that entered through the open door. The room was once again quiet. Exhausted, he slumped to the floor and fell asleep.

The next morning, Nic awakened to the sound of shoveling outside his door. The noise didn't help the pounding of his throbbing headache. Remembering the attack of flying bugs during the night, he opened his door slowly. Thousands of finger-long creatures were climbing over each other at his feet. The sidewalk in front of the two bedrooms was thick with large, squirming bugs.

At first, Nic thought that they must be the bugs from last night's attack, but these creatures didn't have any wings. Tommy motioned for Nic to wait as he shoveled a path down the hallway to Nic's door for Nic to walk through. Nic quickly ran through the mess to join Tommy on clear ground. "I felt like I was in a Hitchcock movie last night," he exclaimed. "Something like the seven plagues revisited."

Tommy looked at Nic and smiled. He enjoyed Nic's theatrical reactions to his first-time experiences. "Our absentminded guest, Bill, left his lantern on," he calmly explained, pointing to the culprit hanging on the hook. "These are the famous termites of Africa that live in those tall mounds that you've seen in the fields. After a rain, they swarm to any light they can find and mate in the air. Then they drop their wings and fall to the ground, hoping to burrow and lay their eggs." He carefully dumped a few more shovels full of bugs into a box, filling it close to the top. He put down his shovel and picked up the box. "Unfortunately for this batch, they landed on a cement floor. No burrowing today. Give me a hand with these, will you?"

Nic reluctantly accepted the box of the squirming swarm. Tommy picked up another full box and headed for the courtyard as Nic followed. "Why are they only in the hallway in front of my door?" asked Nic looking back down the hallway towards his room.

"They only gather around light," explained Tommy. "They swarmed around Bill's lantern, which happened to be right next to your room."

"Some flew in my window from the back of the building, too," shared Nic remembering his battle with the winged giants.

"We all had a few visitors," chuckled Tommy. "There are always a few strays that get confused and lost."

Neighbors were gathered outside the gate to the courtyard. They cheered and chanted as the gate opened. Tommy and Nic carried the boxes of squirming termites through the crowd. Nic turned to Tommy. "What's all this about? What are they saying?"

Tommy stopped and placed the box of the swarm on the front driveway, motioning to Nic to do the same. After setting down the boxes, they stepped back as the people gathered in a crowd around the boxes trying to get a handful of the rare treat. "The rain last night was a blessing. They say we have been blessed again as the termites chose us to swarm to," yelled Tommy in a loud voice so that Nic could hear him over the noisy crowd. "It's a rare gift on Christmas morning."

Nic stood amazed. Young and old eagerly pushed their way up to the boxes, reaching a hand inside. Nic couldn't believe his eyes as he witnessed them grabbing the squirming termites and with their heads tilted back, swallowing the bugs alive. He felt nauseous. "What are they doing? This is gross."

Tommy laughed. "The termites are an excellent source of protein and are considered a rare delicacy here."

A small boy ran up to Nic, enthusiastically offering him a lively morning snack.

"Try one," offered Tommy.

Nic looked at Tommy and then at the thick squirming termite dangling from the boy's fingers. Nic couldn't handle even the thought of the termite wiggling down his throat. He turned green, running to the bathroom while holding his mouth. The boy looked at Tommy with a shrug and rejoined the locals, who were enjoying the protein boost by eating fists full of bugs, their celebration for the abundant blessing they have received.

* * *

NIC FINISHED LOADING an old Land Rover for the delivery of food and medical supplies. The beaten-up jeep had no windshield, windows, or doors. Tommy walked up to Nic to bid him farewell. "It's your last run," he said, slapping Nic on the back firmly. "Time sure did fly. Do you think you'll be able to stomach the celebrations this time?"

Nic laughed. "We'll see. The northern tribe has that crazy hippo-skin dish, and there's always my favorite, the Maasai smoothie."

Tommy's eyes opened wide. "You mean the ritual blood from the bull mixed with cow milk?"

"Yes, and served in a souvenir gourd of course," Nic responded.

"You don't mean to tell me that you actually drank it."

Nic smirked. "Well, you told me not to offend them. I actually only put it to my lips now and pretend to drink. It works. They cheer as I spill it all over my chin."

Tommy laughed. "Well, travel safely, but remember that upon your return, you only have one more group of new volunteers to train before you head on your journey home."

Nic gave Tommy a firm hug, ready for his last African adventure.

Joy can be real only if people look upon their lives as a service and have a definite object in life outside themselves and their personal happiness.

— Leo Tolstoy

Nic jumped into the dust-ridden jeep and drove off on his last adventure to the open plains of Kenya. Using only his compass and a listing of distances in kilometers, he made his way with the life-saving cargo. The brown grass of the plains covered the ground like plush carpeting. It blew in the gentle breeze as herds of zebra, wildebeest, and antelope shuffled across the horizon. As he drove across the plains, Nic spotted a lioness making a gazelle kill and pulled over to observe about thirty yards away. Once the kill was secured, the lioness left, and a majestic lion approached to enjoy the feast. Nic had seen this before, but each time it was as if it was his first. He used to feel bad for the victim, but came to understand that this was a part of life on the plains. Every animal helped the other animals in some way. After enjoying his feast, the lion meandered toward Nic's jeep.

Nic sat totally still, not even blinking. Lazily, the lion laid himself down in the shadow of the jeep, enjoying the only spot of shade for miles. The lion lounged on the ground only a three- or four-foot reach from Nic, dragging his tongue around his blood-stained mouth. Nic knew that the lion was satisfied and, unless threatened, had no reason to attack him since they ate only about once a week. Even though Nic knew this, he still moved cautiously. His jeep did not have a windshield or doors for protection. He moved slowly as he took his camera out of his backpack. The lion turned his head and blinked hard at Nic with his sleepy eyes. Nic froze for a moment. The lion looked away, and Nic held up his camera, taking a few photos of the beautiful animal's profile. The lion almost seemed to pose willfully, unfazed by the clicking of the shutter that echoed across the field. Nic slipped his camera back into the backpack, started up the old rumbling jeep, and pulled away from the lion. Too full to move, the lion just turned his head, looking at Nic as if to say, "Hey, come back with my shade."

Nic plowed through the open bush most of the day and eventually came across a cluster of thorn trees where giraffe meandered around, nibbling on the juicy leaves. Jeeps and faded-camouflage green tents littered the shaded area created by the trees' canopy, creating a camp for what Nic soon discovered to be an international medical-supply team. Stopping to take a break, Nic pulled up to the camp where thirty volunteers were busy unloading supplies into a storage facility just beyond the tree cluster. Nic knew that facilities like this had been set up in remote areas of the bush, their discreet position chosen so that paramilitary or military groups didn't steal the supplies that the volunteers routinely delivered to the tribes as an act of charitable giving. Periodically, they moved the facilities around, usually leaving them in one place for three to six months.

"Americans?" Nic asked.

A young man unloading a pick-up truck replied. "You bet. What are you doing out here on your own?"

"I'm making food and medical-supply deliveries to the tribes. I've been delivering for a few months. This is my last delivery. I'll be heading back to the States soon."

The young man finished unloading his truck and began to carry the boxes to a large tent.

"Let me help you," offered Nic as he jumped out of the jeep. He picked up a box and followed the relief worker to the tent. Another man greeted them, opening the boxes as they were set down.

"Oh no. They did it again." he groaned in disgust.

"Did what?" Nic asked.

The man shook the other boxes around him. "They sent us another large shipment of syringes with no vaccine."

Nic tried to offer encouragement. "Can't you request a shipment of vaccine? The syringes will last until it gets here."

The man looked irritated. It was clear this wasn't the first time he had run into this problem. "Yes, we can make a request, but with no real center to organize all the relief, we pretty much just have to take what we get. The problem is the syringes rust quickly and then are of no use."

"So what do you do with them?" Nic asked, mentally counting the many boxes.

"They get buried in shallow graves like that one over there along with the other supplies we can't use," the man said pointing to a distant field. He shook his head and gently kicked one of the boxes as he walked away. Nic walked with him, still searching his mind for an answer to the problem. "Hey, if you want, you can set up camp over there," said the man to Nic, pointing toward a fire pit. "Our tent is to the left side of the fire."

Nic returned to his jeep and reluctantly pulled out his gear to set up camp near the fire. He added a blanket to the clothesline surrounding the camp, as did the others in the camp. Nic had learned that this practice was essential for shielding the fire from rhinos, who are the firefighters of the African plains. When they see a fire, they go running into it, stomping it out with their large feet. It's not a pleasant experience being awakened by a stampede of rhino in the middle of the night.

Nic finished his deliveries to the three Maasai tribes on his list. Halfway back to Nairobi, he came across another volunteer camp of tents and supplies, which was much smaller than the camp that he stopped at a few days earlier. Evening would soon be upon him, so Nic pulled up. "Greetings, mind if I camp here for the night?"

"Sure, welcome." answered a young woman from the team. "Where are you headed?"

"Back to Nairobi. I'm just finishing a supplies delivery." Nic looked around. "Wow, is it ever dry here. This drought is really devastating the region."

"Yeah, it sure is. Seems like the more we do, the more we learn we have more to do. And then our supplies are erratic. Some of the supplies get confiscated, stolen, and put on the black market. Like today, they sent a massive batch of polio vaccine, but no syringes."

Nic's face lit up. "Wait, I just left a place three days away that has syringes, and no vaccine. Maybe you can arrange an exchange?"

The woman looked at Nic like he was crazy. "Hey, great idea," she said a bit sarcastically. "Now consider the fact that the vaccine was held up in customs for several months. The expiration date is today. We are no longer permitted to dispense it after today. We know that the vaccine can be administered after the expiration date and still be effective, but if we use it past the date, we'll get shut down. The government troops are very suspicious of outsiders in this area and watch every move we make."

"So what happens to it?" The woman answered just as Nic expected.

"It gets buried."

Nic's head dropped. "Again? Isn't that hazardous to those in the area?"

"Yes," she replied, "but we don't have a choice. We have no way to safely dispose of it. We are so short-handed here, and the line of people waiting for services gets longer and longer every day. We don't have anyone to get those syringes anyway. Six days is too long to go short-staffed."

Nic couldn't stop thinking as he set up his camp. His thoughts continued into the evening. He sat on a stool near his small fire, poking the pile of flaming wood with a stick. Mesmerized by the flames, his thoughts deepened, searching for the solution to the unfortunate events of the day. "There has to be a way to organize the relief areas around the world," puzzled Nic. "If only relief agencies could collaborate and utilize relief materials more effectively." As he poked the fire, Nic didn't notice the flames gradually gaining height and strength. He sighed. "I wish this was a world where the primary focus is to take care of each other, a society with common values that sustain this world and its people." A small herd of passing gazelle leapt by, taking Nic's eyes off of the growing fire. The herd quickly passed by and Nic turned back to the fire. The flames were much higher and stronger than he expected.

"There is a way, Nic," said a voice from the fire.

Nic jolted back away from the flames, dropping his stick. He slowly leaned back towards them. "Michael, is that you?" He could see the face of the archangel peering through the dancing flame

"Yes Nic, I am in these flames, just as I am in the flame that fuels your desire to help the people of this world."

"But it's impossible," stammered Nic.

"Look at the stool that you are sitting on. How many legs does it have?"

Nic inspected the seat beneath him. "The stool has three legs."

"And why do you suppose it has three legs?"

Nic scowled a bit, finding Michael's question to be silly. "So it's balanced. So it can support me and not fall over."

"Yes, three legs do not wobble. They remain a consistent and solid foundation to build upon. Such is the foundation of social sustainability."

Nic had certainly heard of environmental sustainability, but *social* sustainability was a new idea.

"There are three core values of social sustainability that can keep a society balanced like the three legs of your stool. These core values are *life*, *equality*, and *growth*."

"But how can these values be present at the same time?" said Nic. "Right now it seems like only the middle class and the rich have abundant life and the opportunity for real personal growth. Most of the world's people are very poor. Grinding poverty deprives them of health and life, let alone any chance at self-realization."

"Even so, Nic, I want you to always remember. The world you have wished for can be attained with a movement for social sustainability based on these three essential principles. It can and it will be done, with your help."

The flames of the fire began to lower.

"Social sustainability emerges when each person fully understands these three core values and consciously lives to fulfill them so that all citizens have equal access to education, robust health, and a full life. This approach is naturally inclusive of environmental sustainability, but it goes far beyond that goal. The three values are universally valid for all people of all races, ethnic groups, nationalities, and cultures. In a sustainable society, all social organizations, whether they are families, businesses, or government agencies, have the intention to support the environmental and social sustainability of the individuals and communities they serve."

"And a world like this is possible? Tell me what I can do to make this happen."

"We must acknowledge that we are all of one Creator. We are all siblings." The strength of the fire began to weaken. The vision of Michael began to fade.

"Wait, I need help. I can't create a sustainable world by myself."

"You will find your help very soon . . ."

Michael's voice weakened and then vanished as if he was pulling back slowly into another dimension. The fire returned to a small flickering flame. Nic picked up the stick he had dropped and returned to absentmindedly poking the fire. His mind swam with visions of a socially sustainable world. "Social sustainability," muttered Nic. "I hope Michael is sending me a lot of help. I'm really going to need it."

The pain of parting is nothing
to the joy of meeting again.
—Charles Dickens

The courtyard had been set up as a casual classroom for a training session for the new volunteers that had just arrived at the Dandora complex. Nic sipped on a glass of water as he sat with Tommy while reviewing his notes in preparation for his last training session. "It would have been nice if I had had one of these training sessions when I arrived here." Nic nudged Tommy with his elbow. "Instead you threw me out to the lions in a rickety old jeep with nothing but a compass."

Tommy laughed. "Yes, your suggestion to hold a training session for new volunteers was a good one." He put his arm around Nic and gave him a slight squeeze. "You survived just fine out there. You wouldn't have listened to anything anybody told you anyway. You would have done it your way and you know it."

Nic gave Tommy a sarcastic scowl. He knew Tommy was right.

A record fourteen new volunteers sat on wooden chairs in uneven rows on either side of a smoldering fire. They were chatting loudly among themselves, eager for instruction. Most were from the USA. One of the volunteers seemed to be getting more attention than the others. Nic couldn't help but notice her himself. She had long, beautiful, dark brown hair and a wide bright smile. She looked similar to the grown-up Sara that Nic often saw in his imagination. A golden sparkle on her cheeks caught Nic's eye. He was mesmerized by her confident smile.

The silence of the group broke through Nic's daydream as he became acutely aware that the group was eagerly focusing in on him. He looked around at the students and then at Tommy, whose raised eyebrows were screaming, "You're on, Nic."

Nic took one more sip of water, cleared his throat, then stood up to introduce himself. "*Jambo* everyone," he began. "My name is Nic, and I've been here for three months doing what many of you will be doing soon. One of my last duties is to conduct this training session for you. Let's start by taking turns sharing a bit about ourselves with the group. We'll start with answering the question: 'What is your name and why are you here?'"

Intentionally, Nic gestured to the dark-haired girl.

"Let's start with you," he said reaching towards her.

The pretty girl waved to everyone. "My name is Sara. I am from Sarasota, Florida."

Nic felt his face flush. *Sara? Is it possible*? But the possibility left as quickly as it came. *This Sara is from Florida, not Pennsylvania. It couldn't be her. Stop being so ridiculous. But wait a minute, Sara moved to Florida when her mother married, right?*

Sara continued. "I'm here because I believe in the power of giving. When I was a child, my mother and I lived in Pennsylvania. We were destitute, and my mother couldn't afford a coat for me. The winters were very cold, so I wasn't allowed to play outside without one. One Christmas I received a gift from Santa Claus. It was a winter coat in a beautifully wrapped box that seemed to have just appeared." Sara flashed a glance at Nic. "Great things can happen if you just believe."

Nic couldn't believe his ears. His jaw dropped. "Oh God!" he blurted. "It's impossible. Sara from Williamsport. Is it really you?"

Sara smiled. She didn't seem to be surprised.

They ran to each other for a long embrace, paying no attention to the confusion of the volunteers around them. As Nic held Sara tightly, he peered over her shoulder and noticed the fire. The fire was blazing brightly, dancing with the delight of heaven, the rippling flames spiraling upward while emitting what seemed to be gold, red, blue, and green crystals. In the flames, Nic faintly saw Nicholas and Michael exchanging a high-five handclap in celebration of the reunion of Nic and Sara. Recognizing his old friends immediately, he smiled through his tears of joy. He also thought he saw a third, unfamiliar figure joining in on the celebration. Nic blinked a few times, assuming the tears in his eyes were distorting his vision. But the new, mysterious figure was *still* there.

Tommy walked up and placed his hand on Nic's shoulder. Nic had shared his memories of Sara with Tommy and his hopes of someday seeing her again. Nic pulled his attention away from the fire.

Tommy offered, "I'll take over from here, Nic. Why don't you two go get reacquainted?"

Nic and Sara stepped back from their embrace and looked at each other. The sparkle in their eyes was bright enough to light up the darkest night. It was as if their childhood connection had never been severed.

Look at her, thought Nic ecstatically. *She's like an angel.*

He held out his hand, and Sara, lifting her weak arm, placed her hand in his. Side-by-side, they silently walked through the gate and began to stroll around the center together. Nic held her hand firmly. He couldn't believe it was really her. He finally broke the silence, turning to her and looking deeply into her eyes. "It's been so long. I thought I'd never see you again. But somehow I always knew I would." He noticed how small and weak her hand felt in his. "All that mattered to me back then was just spending time with you." Nic's crystal blue-green eyes continued to sparkle with a magical glow.

Sara beamed at him. She too had felt the magic of their connection throughout the years. "I loved spending time with you too, but then I had to move away. I was so young and didn't know how to keep in touch. I thought maybe you had forgotten about me."

Nic rolled his eyes. "I've never forgotten you. I never stopped thinking of you. What a crazy miracle to find you here like this." He thought about how often he must have remembered Sara through the years.

"Yes, it *is* a miracle," said Sara, looking up into his eyes.

They continued to walk slowly together and came across a short stone wall towards the back of the complex. They sat down together against the wall as if it were a quaint park bench and shared brief outlines of their life's adventures since childhood.

"I could feel that Mr. Grere, your stepdad, was a good man," shared Nic.

"My mother often protected me because of my arm, but my new father taught me to create strength out of my handicap," said Sara looking at her arm. "He convinced my mother to challenge me and let me learn from my shortcomings." Sara smiled at the thought of him. "When we first moved to Florida, we went to the beach almost every Sunday afternoon. At first, my mother wouldn't let me go into the water above my knees. She was afraid that I would get caught in a current and wouldn't be strong enough to swim."

Nic remembered the day that she wasn't allowed to play outside because it was too cold.

"One Sunday afternoon," continued Sara, "the three of us were sitting in our beach chairs enjoying the sunshine and the warm breeze. My stepfather asked me if I wanted to go for a swim. He took me by the hand and walked me to the water. I thought a swim meant standing at the shore. The waves were unusually big that day because of a large storm in the Gulf, and I loved feeling the force of the incoming waves crashing against my legs. But we didn't stop at the shore. We kept walking. Before I knew it, the water was flowing over my shoulders and I realized my father was no longer holding my hand." Sara's voice rose in excitement. "I looked back at my mother, expecting to see her running to me in a panic, but she just sat in her beach chair, waving to me with a big smile." She leaned into Nic. "That day, in the salty water, my father talked to me about my handicap and how to use it."

"That must have been so great," whispered Nic as he felt the warmth of Sara's emotions.

"It was," whispered Sara with a far-off look in her eyes. She paused for a moment and then caught herself. She sat straight and continued. "That day I was knocked over by the waves and swallowed a lot of saltwater, but I survived. I always got back up again and learned how to position my body so I could brace myself against the strong waves as they came at me from different directions. My father told me that I would fall many times in life, but I could get back up. There is always a way to face every challenge."

"Fabulous advice, you've been blessed to have that man as your father."

Sara smiled. "Yes, I know. I'm so thankful. Mother is always helping me too."

"Your mother has taken good care of you."

"Oh yes," stammered Sara, as if caught by surprise, "my mother has taken good care of me."

Nic thought about his own father and his parting words of advice. *Don't let your fear keep you from following your heart. And that's how I'm here*, realized Nic.

Sara stood and motioned to Nic. "We should probably get back to the group. I don't want to miss too much."

Nic stood and took Sara's hand. They began a slow stroll back to the courtyard. "Did you go to college?" asked Nic.

"Yes. I went to college in Tampa," answered Sara. "I knew that I wanted to be a physical therapist. I wanted to create strength out of my handicap, just like my father said. My goal has been to help my patients learn how to live with their handicap and to encourage them just as my father encouraged me. I'm thinking about writing a novel about the challenges that I've faced, how I overcame them, and how we can help each other get through the challenges of this life. Your experiences can help others get through the challenges of their own lives." They exchanged a loving smile. "That's enough about me," insisted Sara. "Tell me about what you have been doing in Africa."

Nic began to talk about his adventures in Africa. As they approached the courtyard, the group was still in their seats, listening to Tommy. "I had better take over. Tommy will talk until tomorrow." As he opened the gate, it suddenly hit him. *Tomorrow*! When he was telling Sara about his adventures in Africa, he pictured himself experiencing all of those things with her. He forgot that he was leaving the next day. "Oh no," he moaned. "My extended visa is up, and my reservation can't be changed. I can't stay here with you."

Sara put her finger gently to his lips. "Don't worry Nic," she said calmly. "Now that we have been brought together again, I know we will stay together."

"Oh, Sara. I don't know why, but everywhere I went I saw your face. Now we're finally together, and I have to leave. This isn't fair. Why is this happening?"

"How can this not be fair?" Sara held Nic's face in her hands. "We are together again."

Nic wasn't interested in listening. He was focused on his disappointment in having to leave. He continued to protest. "But I can't believe I have to leave tomorrow."

Nic and Sara spent the night by the fire, sharing and watching the southern stars until the sun rose over the plains. They didn't talk much. Nic just wanted to hold her in his arms and never let go. He was lost deep in thought, trying to come up with a way that he could stay. Unfortunately, there was no possible legal way he could remain in Kenya.

Sarasota, Florida. It sounds like a nice place, and Sara loves it there. There isn't anything keeping me up north. I certainly wouldn't miss the cold and the snow. I could live in the warmth and the sunshine. And best of all, I could be with Sara. Nic tightened his hold on Sara. *Yes, I could do it. I could move to Sarasota.* As he felt Sara's warmth against him, he thought about the many times he imagined what it would be like to be with Sara again. She was only with him in his thoughts, and now he had the chance to really be with her. Nic smiled and shook his head.

Sara looked at Nic and watched his expression. "What is it?"

"Oh, I think I just came up with a way for us to stay together."

"You can stay? How?"

"No, I can't stay. They won't renew my visa another time, and I'm out of time to do it even if they would." He cleared his throat.

He was a little apprehensive about telling Sara that he wanted to move to Sarasota. Maybe she didn't want him to follow her. Maybe she would think he was crazy. Nic's father's words began to echo in his head once again. *Don't let your fears keep you from following your heart.*

"Well," he said softly.

"Yes, what is it?" asked Sara eagerly.

"I could . . ."

"You could what?"

Nic turned towards Sara and took her hands in his. With a deep breath he said, "I could move to Sarasota."

Sara sat for a moment. "Really? Are you really going to move to Sarasota?" asked Sara, the pitch of her voice sounding like a little girl.

"If you don't mind," said Nic lowering his head.

"If I don't mind?" yelled Sara. "Of course I don't mind. That's exactly what you are supposed to do. That would be so great."

"What I'm supposed to do?" Nic's question was quickly interrupted.

Sara threw her arms around him and gave him a firm kiss on the mouth. She sat back, realizing that her reaction may have been a bit too much. "I'm sorry," she stammered.

"Oh, don't be sorry. I was worried that you wouldn't want me to move there."

Sara smiled softly. She looked deeply at Nic and raised her hand to his face, holding it gently. "There is something special about you that my spirit is drawn to. I feel as if we have never been apart, and we are destined to be together."

"I feel the very same, Sara. It's settled then. I'll see you again when you return to Sarasota." The sun continued to rise quickly. "I have to get going. I have an early flight." He had gathered his things the day before, leaving him free to spend the evening with Sara. She handed Nic a folded piece of paper.

"Here are my parents' address and phone number. Give them a call when you get back to the States. They'll help you with your transition. They'll be so surprised to hear from you, Nic. I will try to get in touch with them and let them know that you will be contacting them."

Nic took the piece of paper and put it in the front zipper pouch of his backpack. A loud horn screamed a few beeps. "That's my ride," he said. He looked into Sara's dark eyes. "I don't want to say goodbye. We just said hello."

"It's okay, my dearest Nic. We'll see each other again in a few months."

They kissed goodbye in a long embrace surrounded by a golden glow, the warmth of Mt. Kilimanjaro's rising sun kindling their love.

* * *

THE DAY OF SARA'S RETURN arrived. Nic and Sara's mother waited at the airport, anxiously awaiting her return from Africa. Sara's airplane landed on time, and Nic waited impatiently as people began to disembark. The crowd continued to trickle out, embracing those there to welcome them. Nic couldn't wait to hold Sara in his arms. Bouncing on his toes, sifting his eye through the passengers, he looked for her. Finally, there was no one but the flight crew left. Nic and Sara's mother stood frozen, waiting for one more traveler to come through the tunnel. Nobody came. They looked at each other in unspoken fear.

"I'll check with one of the flight attendants," Sara's mother finally said. She approached one of them and asked, "Is there anyone else getting off this flight? I'm expecting my daughter." The attendant replied, "That's all of us. Are you sure you have the right flight information?"

Nic knew the attendant's answer by the look on Sara's mother's face. He walked up to her, taking her hand. "I haven't heard anything from Sara since last month, just like you. The last news we had was she would be on this flight."

Turning to Nic, Sara's mother asked with a quiver in her voice, "What do we do now?"

"I'm going to start making phone calls to track her down," answered Nic quickly. "It may take some time with the connections being so rough, but I'm sure she's all right. Maybe she missed her flight, and she is on the next one. Stay here and wait. I'll check on some other flights."

Sara's mother paced the airport floors watching for any new flights coming in. Hours passed. "I'm beginning to wonder if someone should be at home in case she calls."

Nic agreed. "Why don't you go home and call me if you hear from her."

"Thank you, Nic," she said fighting back a tear. "I'll be talking to you soon. I want you to know that I see how much you care for her. I know deep down in my heart, even with her handicap, that she's going to be all right."

Nic looked at her abruptly. "What handicap?"

Sara's mother smiled. "I know she hides it well, but her arm is deformed."

Nic sighed with relief. "Oh, that's right. You know as children I never really paid attention to it. Only in Africa did I notice it." He put an assuring arm around Sara's mother. "She's a very strong woman. We'll find her and soon." Sara's mother could only smile to hold back the tears.

Nic escorted her to the exit. He turned around and blankly glanced around the airport. After checking again on flight information with the airport personnel, he continued to try numerous times to call Nairobi to see if she had left as scheduled. The lines were always busy or down. He sat on the floor of the crowded waiting area trying to come up with his next move. Finally, he decided to go home. It was getting late, and Nic was exhausted from the hours of emotion and stress. "I'll find her," he told himself as he drove away from the airport. "I have to find her. I can't lose her again."

9

Love is heard in the voice of joy.
—Hawaiian proverb

Nic walked into his apartment and stood for a moment, motionless in the dark. He glanced at his answering machine, hoping to see the light flashing indicating a message. "No messages," he grumbled. "She hasn't called." He stumbled to his bedroom and threw himself on his bed. He laid on his back staring at the ceiling without blinking. "Now what do I do?" He reached out and turned on the lamp on the nightstand. Next to the lamp was his journal and a pen. Nic picked them up and sat down on his bed. Laying his journal on his lap, he opened the tattered book to the first available blank page. He began to write, his thoughts scattering wildly in his mind.

There's so much suffering, so much pain. We have so much here, we just don't realize how bad so many have it in this world. Will it ever change? I feel so guilty to have so much. The social sustainability that Michael talked about seems impossible.

Nic paused, thinking about the night Michael appeared in the fire and talked as if social sustainability really was possible and his promise to send help. Nic shook his head as if it would clear his mind, and then continued writing.

Years of wondering, dreams of our reunion, a one-night dream come true. Feeling lost with the thought of losing her again. Not again Lord, not this time, not this way please. I was hoping today would be a turning point for me, a new beginning in my life. But now, I've lost her again, alone and handicapped, in such a dangerous place, we may have all lost her this time.

He wiped the dampness from his eyes.

It's all my fault. I know I should have stayed to help her get back. I should have stayed to protect her—I'm certain of that now.

Nic was finding it hard to stay awake. His despair exhausted him. He closed his journal and set it back on the nightstand, turned off the light, and fell asleep. As his eyes closed, the tears that welled in his eyes sparkled as they rolled down his cheek.

"You have not lost her, Nic," whispered a voice in the dark. "The next tears that you will shed will be tears of joy."

Nic got up early and continued to try to track down Sara. He sat at his desk trying over and over again to call Tommy in Kenya. As he waited for the operator to once again attempt to put through his call, Nic chewed on a dry bagel, washing it down with a gulp of strong espresso. Finally, the call went through.

"Yes, Yes," Nic yelled in the phone. The operator responded, "Please hold, we are still connecting . . . Sorry sir, it looks like we lost them again . . . Wait a minute, we're in. You're connected now. Go ahead."

Nic jumped to his feet. "Thank you for all your help. Tommy?" A faint voice responded.

"*Jambo*, this is Tommy."

Nic yelled into the phone. "It's Nic, can you hear me all right?"

Tommy answered. "Yes, is something wrong? You sound frantic."

"It's Sara, she didn't show up as scheduled. Is she still there?"

For a second, Nic thought he lost the connection.

"No, I'm sorry Nic. She left here more than a week ago. She changed her flight to fly out of Cairo, Egypt, because she wanted to travel up the Nile for a few days."

"Up the Nile. Is she crazy? Was she alone?" Nic realized that he was yelling into the phone.

Static started increasing on the line. Tommy's voice faded. "What was that Nic? I'm losing . . ." The line went dead.

Nic slammed down the phone. *Now what? I have to go to Egypt?*

The doorbell rang. "I can't be bothered right now. Go away!" He stomped to the door in a rage and opened it forcibly, banging it into the wall. Standing there startled was Sara. Nic focused on his visitor. He felt as if he was melting. "You're alive, my God, you're alive!" Nic jumped through the doorway to embrace her. Tears of joy filled his eyes. Over Sara's shoulder, Nic saw the blurry image of Nicholas and Michael watching from across the street. Nicholas smiled and winked.

Nic smiled back, embracing Sara even harder. A third figure joined Nicholas and Michael, the same figure he saw in the fire when he first saw Sara in Africa. It was a strange woman. *Who is that?*

Sara pulled away, a bit overwhelmed by his greeting. "My mother said I needed to come over right away, but I had no idea you'd be this frantic."

Nic took a deep breath. "Frantic and worried sick at the thought of losing you."

Sara smiled, pleased with Nic's deep devotion. "I tried to call but couldn't get connected long enough and then I was stuck on flights getting here. But everything's all right. We're together now."

Nic grabbed Sara by the arms and pulled her inside his small apartment. He closed the door and dropped to his knee, taking Sara's hand. Taking another big deep breath and looking deeply into her eyes he whispered, "Marry me."

Sara pulled on her ears. "What was that? I think my ears are still clogged from the cabin pressure."

"MARRY ME."

Sara stepped back, releasing his grip. "Are you crazy?" She started to laugh uncontrollably.

"Yes I am. MARRY ME!" Nic abruptly took Sara's hand again and looked into her eyes. Her laughter deflated into a small smile. "Your father has given you wonderful advice to live by," Nic said calmly. "His advice has guided your journey in life. My father advised me to not let fear keep me from following my heart." Nic looked deeply into Sara's warm brown eyes, which started to well with tears. Nic began to worry. *Are these tears of joy or disappointment? Is she already committed to someone else*? His hopes continued to spiral. Nic composed himself. "Sara, I can feel it in my heart that there is a special spiritual connection between us. It's hard to explain, but it feels as if a heavenly force has brought us together. My love for you is deeper than I could ever imagine." He stepped close to Sara and kissed her softly on her cheek. He then stepped back and waited for an answer. Sara stood still for a moment, her eyes sparkling like a crystal in a ray of sunshine.

"Well," she let the sarcasm flow, "I am just as crazy as you are."

Nic shifted on his feet, not knowing what to expect next. Sara reached out with her good arm and gave Nic a sturdy slap on his shoulder. "You don't get it, do you?" she said rolling her eyes with a smile. Nic's expression never changed.

"She will marry you, Nic. And she will help you," whispered a female voice in his ear. Nic stared at Sara, confused by the unfamiliar voice.

"Yes, yes, I will," said Sara, with a radiant and confident smile.

Sara's answer cleared his confusion. He didn't realize that she really wasn't answering Nic. She was agreeing with the voice in his ear.

* * *

NIC FINISHED WRITING NOTES on the board for his students. He had found his niche teaching theology at a small local high school shortly after he and Sara were married. His firsthand experiences in third-world countries drove his passion to teach young people about the full picture of the human condition in the world. His concern for the wellbeing of the world's children had grown since the birth of his two sons. He put down the chalk and turned toward his class.

"Okay. Let's review for the final exam. There you go," he said, pointing to a list on the board. "These are the three reasons people offer to help others." Nic gestured towards the list. "Pragmatic Approach, Religious Approach, and Humanitarian Approach." Nic slid his hand down the list as he read each one. He then turned and pointed to the class. "Examples please." An eager girl in the front row shot her hand up in the air. "Yes, go ahead, Jennifer."

"People who are logical think that we must help others to protect our American lifestyle. We are a minority enjoying a higher standard of living than others. With the army of China twice the size of the U.S. army, many feel we have to provide assistance so we can protect what we have. This is an example of the pragmatic approach."

"Very nice, Jennifer," Nic commended with a nod. "Another example? Go. James." Nic pointed to a boy towards the back of the room.

"People feel obligated to help others and do it for spiritual reasons or for the hope of eternal gain. This demonstrates the religious approach."

"Excellent." Nic turned and pointed to the third example written on the board. "One more, folks. Who has it? Go, Sarah."

Sarah paused a moment to gather her thoughts and then explained. "The last example is those of us who feel we must help our fellow humans since we all share membership in the human family, and that's the humanitarian reason."

"Very good everyone. I think you've got those down pretty well. Now let's take a look at the status of children around the world." Nic stepped to his desk and picked up a manila folder. He opened it and instructed the students to write down the information he was about to tell them. Nic cleared his throat and began to read. "The World Health Organization reports the following: Over nine million children die each year from preventable or curable diseases. That's more than twenty-six thousand a day. The five main killers are pneumonia, over 2 million a year; diarrhea, nearly 2.5 million; malnutrition, 1.7 million; measles, 1.5 million; and malaria, 1.3 million."

A student interrupted by raising his hand.

"Jason?"

"Is that million 'cases' a year?" Jason asked.

Nic shook his head with a stern no. "That's deaths a year."

Jason put his pen down. "Come on, that many dying from diarrhea alone?"

Some of the students laughed. Nic agreed. "Yes. As ridiculous as it sounds, it's true. When we get diarrhea, we take a spoonful of medicine and order a pepperoni pizza with sausage. Malnourished people dehydrate and die, especially if they are children."

"So all they need is anti-diarrhea medicine, and they stay alive?" Jason asked.

Nic smiled. "They actually need something far more effective and inexpensive. It's called ORT or Oral Re-hydration Tablets, which are salt and sugar pills—sugar for energy to recover, and salt so that the cells in the body retain water. That's it, cheap and easy to deliver and administer."

Another student raised her hand. Nic pointed at her. "Yes, Kristanne?"

"So why aren't they getting the supplies?" she asked innocently.

Nic sighed. "Distribution is the major obstacle here. Too many relief supplies get confiscated, sold on black markets, or held from regions that are not politically or religiously aligned with the governing body. That's done in order to force them into submission."

"Isn't malaria carried by mosquitoes?" Kristanne continued. "Wouldn't mosquito repellent take care of that?"

"Yes, but more effective and cheaper are nets to cover their beds at night. Now, let's get an even clearer picture of the status of the human race. These are based on 1990 sources."

Nic redirected the class's attention to the board as he turned to write.

80% live in substandard housing.

80% live in poverty.

75% are illiterate.

65% have never used toilet paper.
50% are malnourished.
70% use unsafe drinking water.
25% have no electricity at all.
7% have a college education.

"The globe's richest 1% owns and controls 50% of the world's wealth."

The class was silent, absorbing the statistics.

"Quite a sorry state, I must admit." Nic strolled among the desks, gaining the attention of each student. "Now, look around at each other and realize that every person in this room, one hundred percent of us, live in the top fraction of the top one percent of the world's population in terms of our standard of living, our health care, and our education." Nic returned to the front of the classroom and faced the students. "Don't just ask why. Ask what are we going to do about it." He paused and then took his seat at his desk. "Any other questions, class?"

Another student raised his hand.

"Yes, Jeremy?"

"Mr. Perugino, do you still play Santa?" Some of the kids chuckled.

Nic knew the student was trying to distract him from any further teaching during the last few minutes of class, but he didn't mind. This was a topic Nic was happy to talk about.

"Absolutely, this is my twentieth anniversary playing the jolly 'ole elf."

Jeremy laughed. "Twenty years. How much longer do you think you'll be doing this?"

Nic shook his head smiling. "A very long time. You see, I plan on becoming Santa when I grow up."

"Aren't you a bit old to believe in fairy tales?" added another student. The students laughed.

Nic answered confidently. "It's not a fairy tale. You see, Santa Claus is real. The first Santa was named Nicholas, who lived in the fourth century in a region of current-day Turkey called Myra. His feast day is December 6. On this day, children from all over the world put out a shoe in the hope that Nicholas will fill it with treats. He later became a respected and legendary figure of Russia and Greece because of his works of charity, especially for his devotion to protecting children from abuse, starvation, and slavery.

Centuries later, Dutch settlers coming to America brought with them Saint Nick's tradition of secretly sharing gifts on the eve of Christmas. The English settlers gave him the name we use now, Santa Claus, from the Dutch name *Sintir Klaas*, which was how the Dutch rendered the name Saint Nicholas from the original Greek." Nic glanced again at the clock, knowing that the bell was about to ring. He continued speaking a bit more quickly. "A famous poem called *'Twas the Night Before Christmas* describes the jolly 'ole elf and how he dressed. Coca-Cola even helped create the current Santa look by painting him on their cans back in the 1930s. Santa is real and constantly evolving."

The anticipated bell ended Nic's Santa Claus tale and marked the beginning of a two-week Christmas break from school. The students left the classroom quickly, eager to celebrate their freedom. The closing classroom topic made Nic extra eager to get home himself. It was time for his yearly transformation.

✷ ✷ ✷

THE NEIGHBORHOOD WAS GLOWING with what seemed like millions of lights and displays. Palm trees were outlined in colorful lights, nativity displays adorned the lawns, and replicas of Santa and his reindeer could be seen mounted on roofs. Nic pulled up to a crowd of neighbors assembling at a home just two houses down from his. "Looks great, everyone," complimented Nic.

Al, a neighbor who had been crowned the decorating coordinator because of his extravagant Christmas displays, waved with his free hand while he held a ladder steady with the other. Al began decorating the outside of his house the weekend after Thanksgiving. His garage was like Santa's workshop where he fashioned figures out of wood. A life-size Santa's sleigh and reindeer was his project last year. This year he added a small choir of angels.

"Santa, are you all set to arrive at seven o'clock tonight?" Al yelled to Nic. "This is going to be the best year yet with all these lights."

"I think we've set a new record this year," Nic agreed. The neighborhood looked like a piece of heaven lit up like a bright cosmos.

Nic headed home and entered his house to the screams of his two energetic young boys. The oldest, Pablo, and his younger brother, Marco, had been born nineteen months apart. Pablo had dark hair like Sara and Marco had blonde hair like Nic, but they both sparkled with Sara's brown eyes.

"So how is my favorite family today?" Nic too was caught up in the excitement.

Sara gave him a kiss and a hug. "All doing very well and excited about Santa's visit tonight."

The boys ran up and hugged Nic's legs, almost knocking him down with their loving force. Nic squatted down to give the boys a hug, but they had already returned to running around screaming. "Yes, I think the whole neighborhood shares the excitement," laughed Nic, covering his ears from the screams.

Sara and the boys helped Nic suit up. Nic and Sara had explained to four-year-old Pablo and three-year-old Marco that Nic always helped Santa each Christmas. After all, Santa was very busy. He didn't have time to come to their neighborhood for an evening. Nic turned up the volume on the CD player as John Lennon's "And So This Is Christmas" boomed through the speakers.

"How long have you been suiting up to this song?" asked Sara, humming along.

Nic smiled. "Since 1975, this song was playing on the radio the very first time I tried on this suit that my mother made for me. I've been playing it ever since while I suit up. Wow, that was twenty years ago."

Sara helped straighten the fluffy wig. "I have a feeling it will be for some time longer, my dear Santa," she said with a sparkle in her eyes.

"Time for the boys to paint my eyebrows white." He bent down for the boys to trace his eyebrows. The boys each took a white make-up crayon and tried to neatly trace Nic's eyebrows.

Sara shook her head. "Nice work, boys." She took the crayons from their small hands while they were still drawing. "But I think we need to clean this up just a bit." With a loving touch, Sara wiped the brows with a damp cloth. "Perfect."

Nic stood up and turned to look in the mirror. "Thank you, Sara. I'm so glad you found this clown makeup for the eyebrows. The white paint I used last year looked great, but . . ."

Sara's eyes got big. "It stayed on for three weeks."

Nic laughed. "Was it really that long?"

Sara straightened his cap. "You look great."

Nic looked in the mirror, inspecting the completed Santa image. "Now if only I could grow a beard," Nic observed as he ran his hand over the fake whiskers. He turned to the side, displaying his protruding belly, making note that he didn't need as much padding this year as he usually did. "I don't think I'll have trouble with the tummy being like a bowl of jelly with your great cooking," he said while patting his bulging stomach. He checked himself in the mirror one more time. "Santa is ready," he announced. "You and the boys can go now. My sleigh should be here in five minutes." Nic leaned over the best he could to talk to the boys. "But before you go, I need help to practice my ho-ho-ho." In unison, they all took a deep breath and bellowed a hearty "HO-HO-HO!"

Sara gave Nic a hug. "See you there, Santa. By the way, you jolly 'ole fool," Sara leaned over to kiss Nic on the cheek. She had a hard time finding a spot with the wig and beard covering his face. "I love you."

Santa slipped out and entered a horse-drawn carriage just behind his house that had been prepared for him by some of the dads in his neighborhood. He mounted the carriage and soon emerged from around the corner to a crowd of cheering families in a different part of his neighborhood than in his afternoon encounter. Nic climbed out as gracefully as he could.

"Ho-ho-ho! Merry Christmas everyone!" he shouted in his deep Santa voice. "Merry Christmas!" Nic waved and greeted the crowd of screaming children and cheering adults. Al led him to a spot lit chair on the front porch. The children ran up to Santa but were quickly controlled by neighborhood teens acting as Santa's elves.

"Line up if you want to see Santa," yelled one of the elves. The children quickly shoved themselves into a line, their parents trying to keep them orderly, holding tight to their cameras and video recorders.

After the first few children, Santa gleamed as the children next in line approached him. Pablo and Marco walked timidly to their daddy. Although they knew it was him, the lights added an eerie glow to his face and the chaos around them was unnerving. Sensing their apprehension, Nic spoke gently to them, softening his voice from his usual Santa boom.

"It's all right boys. Come sit on Santa's lap." The familiar voice assured them, and they climbed up on his lap, one on each knee. Nic could feel a tear well up in his eyes. *Twenty years of being Santa. I would have never thought back then that I would be sitting here with my own beautiful children on my lap.*

The elves offered the boys a candy cane. Marco took it happily but Pablo hesitated. He turned to look at Nic, asking him with his eyes if it is all right for him to take it. Nic looked into Pablo's dark trusting eyes. *They are just like his mother's,* thought Nic with a smile.

Pablo's eyes fixed on Nic's, waiting for an answer. As Pablo's and Santa's eyes met, Pablo's eyes sparkled like crystal in bright sunlight. A warmth poured over Nic. He recognized that sparkle. "Yes, young man," he said softly. "You can take the candy. Enjoy it." Pablo turned quickly and grabbed the candy cane.

"Wait, don't leave Santa's lap yet," yelled Sara, positioning herself to take a picture. "Look this way, boys." After Sara was satisfied with her photos, she helped the boys off of Santa's lap. Before leaving, she turned and sat firmly on Nic's lap, snuggling into his fuzzy suit.

"Merry Christmas Santa," she said sweetly.

Nic smiled.

"Yes, it is. It couldn't be any merrier." Nic wished that Sara could sit with him all evening, but the yelling children reminded him that there were many more anxious visitors waiting in line.

Sara stood and stepped aside, motioning to the next in line to approach the jolly 'ole elf. She stood for a moment, watching her husband enjoying his role. A smile of joy filled her face.

"Do you think he's ready?" whispered a familiar female voice in her ear.

"Yes, he's ready," affirmed Sara, nodding her head.

"How about you? Are you ready?"

"I was born ready," smirked Sara.

"Yes you were," chuckled the voice. "Tonight it begins."

* * *

THE EVENING PASSED by quickly. Nic loved putting on his Santa suit, but equally loved taking it off. He was happy to be out of the hot suit and back into comfortable clothes. He sat back on the couch with Pablo and Marco at his side. Sara handed Nic a small wrapped gift. "Here's an early gift for you dear."

Nic accepted it with a suspicious smirk. He opened the gift with the help of the boys. "'It's *The Santa Clause*, with Tim Allen. I always wanted to see this movie." He flashed Sara a smile. "Perfect after a night like this." Sara returned his smile and put the movie in the VCR.

"I thought you'd like it."

The boys snuggled with their blankets next to Nic. Sara joined them, holding a bowl of popcorn to share. The movie started and Nic was mesmerized as he watched the main character's transformation into Santa Claus, but this transformation was without a wig or make-up crayons. By the end of the movie, the boys had fallen asleep on their parents' laps. Sara looked over at Nic. He was weeping quietly. She raised her eyebrows. "Are you crying?"

Nic sniffled and wiped a tear that had fallen to his cheek.

"This is a comedy," chuckled Sara.

"I know, but I can't help it. He did what I've always wanted to do."

"What do you mean, Nic?" whispered Sara, although she already knew.

"He turned into Santa Claus. The dad actually turned into Santa Claus. Hollywood transformed him."

"You too can write your own movie and can turn into Santa," she said with a smile.

Nic wiped his cheeks. "We've got to get these boys to bed," he said. They gently carried the boys to bed, tucked them in, and walked towards their own bedroom.

"If you work hard enough at it, you might just be able to become Santa," said Sara as they got into bed. "When you grow up, that is."

Nic laughed. "Yes indeed, if I ever *do* grow up," yawned Nic as his head eased into his pillow.

10

Scatter joy!
—Ralph Waldo Emerson

Nic quickly fell into a deep sleep and began to have a vivid dream. He was lying in bed and watching his belly and beard grow before his eyes. Astounded, he ran to peer into the bathroom mirror. Closing and rubbing his eyes in disbelief, he opened them to find himself all suited up and standing in front of a magnificent castle in the North Pole. He was Santa Claus.

A small elf silently tapped his arm. Nic turned to the elf who handed him the reins to a reindeer-drawn sleigh. The sleigh shined with red, blue, and green crystals that highlighted intricate swirling designs on a gold background. He accepted the reins and climbed into the sleigh. The bench was softly cushioned with warm red velvet. Nic settled in and gently shook the reins. The majestic reindeer began to prance with their heads held high. Nic slowly pulled back on the reins, firmly guiding the sleigh up into the air. Nic noticed that somehow he knew exactly what to do. They ascended smoothly into the night sky, moving forward like a paper airplane gliding in a strong breeze. As he enjoyed the view of the castle in the snow just below him, he was nudged roughly. Startled, he turned to see Nicholas sitting next to him.

"Greetings, Nic. You're not bad at this at all. Feels good, doesn't it?"

Nic was ecstatic. "Nicholas!" Nic felt like a young boy who had just met his superhero.

"I've been keeping a close watch on you." Nicholas's eyes sparkled. "It's time to show you how it all got started." Nicholas set his staff between Nic and himself, resting it carefully on the back of the seat. Taking the reins from Nic, he gave them a quick jerk. A strong wind momentarily took Nic's breath away as the sleigh propelled forward.

"Where are we going?" asked Nic as they abruptly changed direction.

"I am taking you on an adventure," said Nicholas. "You like adventures, don't you Nic?"

"Yes, I do," said Nic with hesitation. "What kind of adventure are you taking me on?"

Nicholas chuckled. "Don't worry. You are safe with me."

Nic sat back in the sleigh. They seemed to be moving very slowly now and there was no longer any wind. "Where are we going?" Nic asked again.

"We are going to Myra in the year 340 A.D.," answered Nicholas casually.

"What?" exclaimed Nic. Before he could say anything else, they began to descend rapidly. They approached a simple brick home. The bright moon cut through the dark night, casting a silver glow across its shingled roof. Nicholas pointed down to the chimney.

"See, that's me." Nic saw a young man in a long, red, hooded cape on the roof of the house, hovering over the chimney. "This is the moment when, on Christmas Eve, I dropped three bags of gold coins to save the cobbler's daughters from being taken and sold to pay his rent."

They pulled the sleigh up to the window and peered inside. Three girls were sleeping near a cold fireplace. Nic could hear the bags drop with a thud in the fireplace, waking one of them. The curious girl sat up looking for the source of the sudden sound. Looking inside the dark hearth, she saw the simple red bags tied with strings that were lit up by a beam of moonlight shining down through the chimney. She reached in to retrieve the bags. Opening one of them, she turned it over to reveal its contents. To her surprise, shiny gold coins fell to the floor. She immediately ran to her father yelling in excitement.

Nic smiled. "Many good deeds have been performed in your name because of this. This isn't the only act of charity you performed."

"No, it isn't," agreed Nicholas. "And the joy of it all is how my spirit lives on in so many generous people who give gifts like this during the holidays and throughout the year." Nicholas whipped the reins again, and the strong legs of the reindeer lifted them up as they ascended into the stars. "I am going to take you on a whirlwind trip around the world to show you the spirit of sharing. Hold on, here we go!"

Nicholas threw his hand into the air, releasing a handful of sparkling green, red, and blue crystals. Nic grabbed Nicholas's arm, expecting the jerk of an accelerating sleigh. Instead, they floated slowly to the earth.

The sleigh hovered steadily over a harbor filled with modest fishing boats. The sailors were decorating their crafts with blue and white lights, the colors of the flag of Greece, in honor of the country's patron saint.

"Here I'm known as St. Nicholas," Nicholas explained. "I am the protector of sailors and seamen. Each year, on December 6, I am celebrated for my good deeds on land and as the protector of those at sea." He chuckled. "The Grecian tradition portrays me with soaking wet clothes and a beard that is always dripping with seawater. My face is covered with perspiration from fighting raging storms, rescuing sinking ships, and saving men from drowning."

The Grecian landscape slowly faded as the hills of northeast Europe came into view.

"And in the Netherlands they call me *Sintirklaas*. I am celebrated on Saint Nicholas' Eve."

"Hey, he looks just like you," Nic exclaimed, pointing to a man dressed in red robes surrounded by children. His thick, white, wavy hair and beard resembled the lush whiskers of Nicholas.

"Their portrayal is quite accurate," agreed Nicholas, appreciating the strength and gentleness in the demeanor of the Dutch version of himself. "On the evening of December 6, families in the Netherlands gather to exchange cleverly wrapped gifts, or 'surprises', as they call them. They wrap the gift in order to disguise the contents, therefore surprising the recipient. The Dutch people started that particular tradition, and it's now observed all over the world."

The Nicholas look-alike turned his head toward them. Nic swore that he was looking right at him, but he knew that was impossible. A soft giggle tickled Nic's ears, coming from the staff resting on the seat next to him. Nic looked quickly at the staff, but only saw the residual golden sparkle left from the magical trio of children he had seen once before as a child on Nicholas' staff. The two men continued on their amazing trip as the landscape changed quickly once again.

"In Croatia, I'm *Sveti Nikola*, in Hungary, *Szent Mikulas*, and I'm *Dun Che Lao* in China," continued Nicholas.

At each location, Nic caught a glimpse of that country's version of Nicholas during a brief moment of one of their Christmas celebrations. As they hovered over Greenland, Nicholas pointed out a huge Viking ship floating majestically in its dock.

"Notice the bow," Nicholas pointed out. The image of Nicholas was carved intricately, showing the way.

After another transition, Nic recognized the landscape of Florida, revealing a populated modern city hugging a coastline.

"This port city, now called Jacksonville, was once called Nicholas Ferry Port," shared Nicholas. "Thousands of churches and many parks share the namesake. Even this port was named after me originally."

Nic had to ask, "Of all these traditions and these different beliefs and religions, which one is right?"

With a smile, Nicholas looked away and said, "All of them are. They point to the one true Creator of all. Real religion doesn't belong to any group or organization that is ruled by man-made laws. It's always defined as one's relationship with and deep personal experience of God as you understand God to be. But it's a sad fact that many churches and other Christian groups practice their beliefs in ways that support the greed of their leaders. This gives me a lot of pain."

Nicholas paused. He saw that he had shared enough with Nic, his head no doubt swimming with the amazing things that he had seen and heard. "Come, let us go to another port, the one just below us. I want to show you something else."

They touched down, and Nic and Nicholas stepped out of the sleigh and walked to a nearby port. A boat was leaving the dock, filled shoulder-to-shoulder with people of all ages. At the center of the boat was a tall statue lit by a bright light.

"That's a statue of you, isn't it?" observed Nic.

"Yes, it is," confirmed Nicholas. "My relics, the bones I once used, were brought to this town, named Bari, on May 8, 1087. Each year on this day, the faithful gather and place this statue on a boat that travels around the harbor in front of this small city with many other boats following. This is part of their three-day celebration called *Festa di San Nicola*."

The sleigh appeared next to the two travelers, and they boarded. Nicholas pulled the reins, and it gently ascended back into the night sky.

"These are all beautiful tributes and images of the past," sighed Nicholas. "Waves of immigrants from many countries later came to America, bringing their beautiful traditions and customs with them. But throughout the years, my image has been changed and distorted as you know." Nicholas handed Nic a piece of paper with an advertisement exploiting the image of Santa Claus. On it was a modern picture of Santa Claus promoting a product. "That advertisement symbolizes what has happened to these beautiful images."

Nic shook his head. "Your image has become more and more commercialized."

"Yes, Santa Claus is now used more for profit rather than for charity. Many people still hold dear the tradition of charitable giving at Christmas time, but it's not nearly enough to care for the poor and dying children of the world. Even my own image, the universal symbol of the spirit of sharing, has been tarnished. The rich are getting ever more rich, and the poor are turning even poorer, all over the world. And, the rich people of Earth are also destroying the environment to make even more money, which mostly affects the lives of the poor in every country."

Nic handed the paper back to Nicholas. But before it left his hand, it vanished, leaving behind a cloud of gold dust. He suddenly heard feelings being expressed by the magical trio on the staff. To his surprise, the sounds were not ones of joy or mischief. They were cries of sadness. Nic looked at the staff. The three children were weeping, tears dripping from their usually sparkling eyes.

Nicholas looked sadly at his children, tears also replacing his eyes' own sparkle. Nicholas sighed heavily. "Too many children suffer all over the world. They will get the help they need, very soon. I believe and know they will."

Feeling sad for the children and his friend, Nic was happy to hear that help was on the way. "Who will help the children?"

The face of Nicholas changed from despair to joy. He smiled at Nic. "You!"

"Me?"

"Yes, you. All of you. That's who will be helping."

The children on the staff began to smile with hope. Looking at Nic, they solidified, still wearing their smiles.

"Why are you showing me all of this?" Nic asked.

"To prepare you," replied Nicholas.

"For what?"

Nicholas was surprised. "Your mission, of course."

"Helping people feel the spirit of sharing? The social sustainability that Michael talked about?"

"Yes," said Nicholas, "and to set the record straight."

"Set what record straight?"

Nicholas answered with a question. "What is Christmas all about?"

Nic replied, "Celebrating the birth of the Christ child every December 25."

Nicholas laughed. "The birth of Jesus was actually on August 21, not December 25." Nic looked surprised. Nicholas continued. "The old Roman calendar-makers did not know the day of the actual birth, so they associated it with the winter solstice. It also happened that the Roman festival of Mithra occurred on December 25, so some say they borrowed that date." Nicholas shifted in his seat to directly face Nic. "The actual date is not important, what is truly essential is that we celebrate the day God became human to teach the love of the Creator. Again, Nic, what is Christmas all about, and what is Santa all about?"

Nic's blank expression revealed his confusion. He felt as if he had been given a hundred pieces to a puzzle and he was expected to put them together without a picture to follow.

Nicholas sat back and explained, "On earth, Jesus was the perfectly unified human personality. What was most remarkable about Jesus was not so much his perfection but his remarkable symmetry of character, his exquisite balance of virtues."

He paused so Nic could take it all in.

"His example was not for you to emulate the particular things he did in his life, but rather to live by the same Spirit that He used to conduct his perfect life. Jesus initiated the new and living way for us to become closer to God, sharing the love of the Creator through his Holy Spirit—the spirit of sharing, of courage, and of hope."

Nic sat quietly for a moment, contemplating Nicholas' words. "I still don't see what the birth of Jesus has to do with Santa Claus," he confessed. "And what does it have to do with me?"

"Listen carefully," instructed Nicholas. "On Earth, my life was a mercy mission devoted to sharing the love of Christ. The true Santa Claus is not a person, but he is a reminder to live your life according to the Spirit of Jesus." He turned towards Nic. "Your mission is to rekindle the same spirit of sharing."

Nic was overwhelmed. "Nicholas," he stammered, "I want to save children from dying unnecessarily. I have seen too much suffering, and it's breaking my heart. I just don't know that I am the one for this mission. I don't know how."

"Keep searching, and you will find a way to make it all happen." Nicholas smiled. "Sara has already figured it out. Listen to her."

"When is she going to tell me?" The conversation continued to mystify him.

"She already has," bellowed Nicholas. "Listen to her."

Nic sat quietly, trying to take in all that he had seen and heard.

Nicholas put his arm around Nic's shoulders. "More help is already on the way, son, working to assist you in this mission."

Still uncertain, Nic continued to ask questions. "What kind of help?"

"The Creator has granted my request to send the angels of hope, generosity, and courage to you." Nic's eyes grew large. "When it is time, they will reveal themselves to you and show you what you need to know to rekindle the spirit of sharing."

"When will this be?"

Nicholas nodded calmly. "It will be when it is time."

"What do I do until then?"

Nicholas began to fade, his voice trailed into the night. "Nic, you must learn to listen more to your heart and to Sara. She just told you what to do. Listen to her . . . listen . . ."

Nic abruptly woke up in his bed. He turned to look at the clock's red glow. It was 1:30am. Despite the beautiful visitation, Nic felt annoyed. *Why can't Michael or Saint Nicholas just tell me what to do? Just tell me what to do, and I'll try to do it.* He looked at Sara sleeping peacefully, gently brushing a strand of hair that had fallen across her face. "What did you tell me?" he whispered. He continued to look at her face, trying to recall their conversations the evening before. "We didn't have time to talk very much because of the neighborhood Santa Claus visit," he recalled. "Then we watched a movie together." Nic chuckled at himself when he remembered his emotional display at the end of the movie. Then it hit him. "Sara said to write my own movie. Could that be it?" Nic quickly rolled out of bed and went to his desk. He turned on the small desk lamp, opened a notebook, and was compelled to write. Sara awakened. Seeing that Nic wasn't in bed, she got up and began to look for him, finding him at the desk bent over the notebook, writing intently.

"What are you doing?" she asked with a yawn.

"I had a wild dream that I have to write down. Go back to bed. I'll be there soon."

Sara turned and stumbled back to bed. As she pulled the covers up around her, she whispered, "It has begun, Mother, just like you said."

* * *

SARA WOKE UP to find Nic's side of the bed empty, once again. She walked through the kitchen into the family room to find the now-familiar sight of Nic sitting on the floor in front of the fireplace with a burned-out fire. Crumpled pieces of paper surrounded him. Sara sighed heavily. She walked over to Nic and gently ran her fingers through his tussled hair. "Nic, what's going on in there?" she asked softly, gently tapping his head.

Nic looked up at her, his face haggard. "I'm not sure." He looked back at his notebook, sitting in silence.

Sara squatted down next to Nic. "You have become obsessed with whatever it is you've been doing for a week now. What's going on?"

"It's all your idea."

"My idea? What's my idea?"

"The movie."

Sara shook her head. "What movie?"

Nic pointed to a statue of Santa on the mantle. "About Santa, remember? The night of the neighborhood Santa visit, you said I should write my own movie so that I can become Santa Claus. I went to sleep that night and had a dream in which Nicholas told me to listen to you." Sara dropped down out of her squat and sat on the floor.

"So, that is what you've been doing."

Nic sighed. "I know this might sound crazy, but I am trying to write a movie screenplay treatment. Its story is my vision. It is about the journey of a young man who wants to be a Santa who develops innovative relief programs, traveling around the world working to save children and their families, and at the same time, rekindles the spirit of sharing among the people he meets. We can use the funds to start a global child relief mission that actually implements these programs. I'm thinking of calling the movie *Operation: Santa Claus*. Sara, with the help of this movie, I could actually become a *real* Santa Claus."

Sara put her arm around Nic. Glancing at his notebook she asked, "So what have you got so far? Can I see it?"

Nic held his notebook to his chest. "No. I'm still trying to piece a bunch of ideas together." He put down his notebook. "I'm sorry I've been so out of it lately. This idea has taken all my energy."

"I am here to help, Nic. Let me know what I can do."

Nic stretched his back with a cracking arch. "I love you, Sara," he said offering a peck on her cheek. "You don't think I'm a bit crazy because of this, do you?"

"My dear soulmate, we are in this together. If you're crazy, then I'm crazy too."

* * *

MONTHS PASSED SINCE the screenplay treatment was distributed. Nic sat at the dinner table with his family in disappointment. In his hand was yet another returned envelope containing his treatment. "They won't even look at it," he complained, staring at the red 'return to sender' and 'unsolicited, unopened, unread' stamps on the envelope. "If they would just read the screenplay, they would see how innovative these relief ideas are and they would realize the importance of this project." A minute passed in silence as Nic pushed his food around his plate.

"What about starting it?"

"Start what?" mumbled Nic, slumping into his chair, feeling a bit too defeated to start anything.

Sara paused, listening to a voice from within. "The innovative relief program for children, of course. You've got the plan for it right there in the script. You even have an innovative plan to add parent education to your programs of crisis relief for their children. And your idea of creating a global relief monitoring system is a great way to improve the effectiveness of all the relief agencies out there."

Nic slowly sat up in his chair. "But how?"

"You don't get it, Nic."

Nic wasn't listening to Sara. His mind was whirring with ideas. "I do know a lot of people who run charities right here in town," he said absentmindedly. "I could ask them for advice, and they could show me what to do."

"You have it within yourself, Nic."

Nic still wasn't listening. "We already know how charities work," she added. "We can reach a lot of people, help them, educate them, and spend very little money doing it." He finally broke out of his trance and looked at Sara. "Do you believe it can be done?"

"The question is, do *you* believe?"

"As long as you'll help me."

Sara smiled. "I believe in you." She offered Nic her hand.

Nic took her hand firmly, and they shook in agreement, their eyes sparkling with excitement. "Should we call it *Operation Santa Claus*?"

"Santa Claus?" chimed the brothers together. Nic had gotten the attention of the young boys.

Sara thought for a moment. "It's really all about serving everyone, and we are all children of the Creator. What do you think about *Operation Serving Children*?"

Nic looked at his little boys. Marco was trying to scoop his rice onto his spoon, pushing more rice off of his plate and onto the table than on his spoon. Pablo gulped loudly, enjoying his cup of cold juice.

"Guess what, boys," Nic said with a smile. "Looks like your daddy is going to start a global relief agency. Operation Serving Children."

Pablo's eyebrows furrowed. "What's a 'leafancy'?"

Nic and Sara laughed.

"Relief agency," said Sara, enunciating her words carefully.

"Well," explained Nic, "it's a business where we will collect money and help feed families, get medicine for them, that kind of thing."

"Operate Surfing?" struggled Marco.

"Just say 'OSC'"," guided Nic.

"Can I help too?" Pablo enthusiastically added, "OSC."

"Of course, Pablo. We'll make it our family business to help others," said Nic proudly.

Pablo reached his hand into his pocket and struggled to pull it back out. When his little fist finally emerged, he opened his hand and placed a small plastic deer, a marble, and a dirty nickel on the table. Pablo separated the nickel from the pile. "Here, Daddy," he said pushing the nickel across the table towards Nic. "Here's some money for their food."

Holding the nickel up to the heavens, Nic proclaimed, "Our first donation."

11

Joy lies in the fight, in the attempt,
in the suffering involved, not in the victory itself.
—Mahatma Gandhi

Nic sat in a large boardroom awaiting the arrival of the directors of a committee for the largest funding foundation in Florida. He helped himself to a cup of coffee and sat nervously at the large meeting table.

"They're late." Nic checked the time on his cell phone. A moment later, the committee directors abruptly entered, taking a seat at the opposite end of the long table far away from Nic. Two committee members were present: one an elderly man with a kind, suntanned face who was dressed impeccably, and the other was a woman whose face was hard and expressionless.

Without introductions or even a simple greeting, she began. "We have reviewed your proposal, and we must admit we don't know where to begin."

Nic was hopeful. An opening line like that could only be good. Looking at the papers that Nic submitted, she continued.

"The services you offer local families are already addressed by many other competent and established agencies."

"Do other agencies offer education to help them escape the financial situations they are in?" interrupted Nic.

The woman didn't even look at Nic and continued. "We do not fund services that local agencies already provide."

Nic sat forward, trying to feel closer to his critics. "Who else teaches them financial security and independence so they may never have to call another charity again?"

The woman dropped Nic's papers. "None of them do, but they can do such things—in fact, they ought to—and since they ultimately can, eventually they will, and thus there is no need to fund you."

"What about helping to fund the . . ."

A phone suddenly rang. The elder director casually reached into his pocket and answered his phone. "Rick, so good to hear from you. Are you still free for lunch tomorrow? Excellent. No, no, I'm not busy at all. It's a quiet day. Go right ahead. Nothing important going on here."

Nic diverted his eyes away from him and back to the woman who was glaring at him.

"As I have already stated, we do not fund agencies providing duplicate services. *And* we do not fund movie projects about Santa." She placed the papers in a manila folder and shoved them across the table at Nic. "It's like . . . like you're trying to save the world."

Her accusation caught Nic off guard, but he managed a firm reply. "The world has already been saved, but thanks for the compliment."

He took a deep breath as he stood up to leave. He collected the rest of his papers and waved to the man on the phone, who returned the wave while smiling. The woman continued to glare at him. Nic managed a smiled, thanked her for her time, and walked out the door. He could feel her glare bearing down on him all the way down the hall. It followed him home, shadowed over him throughout the evening, and even penetrated his dreams that night.

The boardroom table in Nic's dream seemed to go on forever. He sat alone at one end, squinting as he looked down the never-ending table that vanished into darkness. He saw no one but could still feel the cold glare that had followed him into his dreams.

"Is anybody there?" he nervously called out into the darkness.

"I am always here, Nic." The familiar voice dissolved Nic's dark feeling. He was relieved to see Michael sitting in a chair near him at the table.

"This just isn't working," mumbled Nic. He turned towards Michael and leaned forward on the table. "I can't do this, Michael."

"Yes you can, Nic," responded Michael calmly

"I wish everyone would stop telling me I can do this," blurted Nic. "Haven't you seen what's been happening?"

"Of course I have. You don't get it, Nic."

Nic's tone reflected his irritation "No, *you* don't get it," he barked as he pushed his chair back and stood tall. He planted his hands firmly on the table and leaned towards Michael. "I don't think you have any idea what I have been going through. You couldn't have seen any of it. If you did, you would know that nothing has been going right ever since we started this charity."

Michael stood slowly. "All right, Nic. Show me."

"What do you mean?"

"What haven't I seen? What happened?"

"Well, first of all, there was the launching of the charity. We worked so hard and got absolutely nothing from it."

"Show me." Michael placed his hands on top of Nic's.

Instantly, Nic found himself standing in a park. He recognized it immediately. He was in the center of St. Armand's Circle, a unique shopping and dining village nestled on a quaint barrier island near Sarasota. The park was encircled by a wide sidewalk lined with exclusive stores and restaurants. The Circle was alive with various organized groups singing Christmas carols, dancing, and steel drummers banging out Christmas tunes.

"This is that day in July when we launched the charity," observed Nic. "We called it 'Christmas in July.' We were hoping to raise a lot of funds to help families and get the word out about Operation Serving Children." A large crowd filled the area, which was unusual, as the summer months consistently saw a drop in patrons.

"Looks like a lot of families are enjoying themselves," said Michael, looking around at the festivities. "I see a lot of smiling faces."

Nic looked suspiciously at Michael. "Sure they enjoyed it, but at our expense. It took a lot of work and money to organize and execute that event."

Around the corner came a horse-drawn carriage carrying Sara, Pablo, Marco, and Nic dressed as Santa Claus. Nic pointed Michael's attention towards it. "We rode in on the carriage, and then I sat on a bench in front of one of the stores and greeted children," commentated Nic as he watched himself disembark the carriage to the delight of screaming children. "I was so hot in that outfit, I was practically seeing stars. Sara was literally running around the Circle checking on each entertainment group, troubleshooting, and making sure everything was running smoothly. That's the night we found out she was expecting. I felt so bad that she was out in the heat all day working so hard."

Nic expected a sympathetic comment from Michael, but he only listened in silence. Nic continued. "It wasn't easy, but I secured a car to raffle. We didn't even sell enough tickets to hold the raffle. We had to return the money to the few that did buy a ticket. A volunteer even spilled a soda on our information pamphlets that they were supposed to hand out to the crowd. Nothing went right."

Michael pointed to Pablo and Marco standing next to Santa with huge grins, obviously proud to be his special elves. "It looks like your boys really enjoyed that day."

"Sure, it all looks nice, and people are having a great time," said Nic. "The businesses loved it. They all had a big profit that day because of the large crowd. But do you know how much in donations the charity received that night?" Nic answered his own question. "Zero. Zip. We got absolutely nothing from that event. We didn't help even one person."

"Nobody got anything from it at all?" questioned Michael.

"We didn't get one penny," scowled Nic. "I was shocked."

"Was Sara disappointed as well?"

Nic thought for a moment. "For some reason, she thought it went well. She just told me, 'Great things take a great time to achieve.'"

"She is very wise," Michael said, placing his hand on Nic's shoulder. "What else has happened?"

Nic thought about the phone call he recently received from the local food bank. Before he could begin his story, he and Michael were standing on a sidewalk in a familiar neighborhood. The street was lined with cars, and people were walking up the driveway to the house in front of him. The garage door was open revealing boxes and boxes of food and supplies. Nic watched himself walk up the driveway to confront Jane, a volunteer he had entrusted to distribute food to local needy families.

"Jane, I received a phone call from the food bank today," informed the Nic in the vision. "They say you're charging enough for food and supplies to take care of over one hundred families a week. I gave you provisions for only twenty families. Why this stockpile here in your garage?" The activity continued as people walked up the driveway and cars tried to find a place to park nearby. Nic glared at Jane.

"Hey Jane," yelled someone from a car slowly cruising by. "What goodies do you have for us this weekend?"

Jane started to panic. "Sorry, folks, there's no shopping today, store's closed," she yelled.

"What do you mean closed?" complained a woman with hands on her hips. "I already paid in advance. I want my food."

Nic shuffled through the copious boxes of supplies that OSC had paid for. He was outraged. "I can't believe it," he repeated to himself. "I just can't believe it." A look of fear and desperation crept over Jane's face.

Nic stepped back to avoid his upset twin-self as he stormed down the driveway to his car. "I was so angry that day," said Nic, feeling the frustration of the situation all over again. "I trusted her."

"Why did you leave in such a hurry?"

"It was Sara. I heard a whisper of her voice in my head saying, 'Walk away.' That's exactly what I needed to do. If I stayed, my anger would have made the situation even worse."

A young woman walked up the driveway carrying a baby on her right hip and toting a toddler by her left hand. She stopped to talk to Jane, her head dropping. She stood for a moment, staring at the ground. She walked away empty-handed.

"It looks like people just wanted food. Isn't that what the volunteer was supposed to do, give people a way to get food who otherwise could not afford it?" asked Michael.

"But the volunteer was profiting from selling the food that I paid for." Nic's frustration was building. "You don't understand. I trusted her and she took advantage of me."

"Was Sara frustrated as well?"

"It didn't seem to bother her," Nic recalled. "I remember her telling me, 'Don't let somebody's bad choice stop you from doing what *you* choose to do.'"

"Again, she is very wise," repeated Michael.

Nic looked at Michael. Disappointment tainted Nic's voice as he continued his grumbling. "And then there's Donna, a volunteer who helped me develop the charity website and do some writing for us. She now claims that she is the author of the new version of the OSC screenplay and that the website is her property, just because she did small amounts of copyediting. I've been advised to legally protect our rights, but it's going to cost about $3,500 to file trademarks and copyrights. It's something that must be done now, or Donna may have a claim on the rights." Nic looked up at the sky and heaved a sigh. "She was a board member and longtime friend." Nic closed his eyes and dropped his head. "We don't have much money left. I've used up all of our retirement accounts."

"What is in all of those bags?" asked Michael.

Nic raised his head and opened his eyes. They were no longer on the sidewalk in front of the volunteer's home, but back in Nic's home. Sara was carrying a box into the house from the garage. She set the box down and placed her hands on her expanded waist. "We are starting to run out of room," she announced. "This is family number 149," she said with a smile as she picked up an application. She studied the form and began to wrap gifts for the family.

"Those are bags of gifts that we delivered to families during the holidays," said Nic pointing to the collection of white plastic bags, all neatly filled and marked with each family's name, address, and ages of children.

"149 families. That's quite a few, don't you think?"

"I guess so," shrugged Nic, "but it isn't enough. If I had more money and better support I could do so much more."

"You talk as if you have done nothing."

Michael walked closer to Sara. "Sara seems to be content."

Nic gave Michael a puzzled look. "You keep focusing on Sara. What about *me* and what *I've* been going through?"

"Sara understands. Listen to her."

"I *am* listening to her, but it isn't working. What am I supposed to do?" Nic peered at the dream-version of Sara, searching for an answer to his question.

She smiled at Nic. "It's time, Nic. It's time, it's time . . ."

"Nic, it's time to get up." Sara gave Nic a nudge. "You asked me to make sure you got up early so you can prepare for today's board meeting. It's time."

Nic slowly opened his eyes to Sara standing at his bedside.

Sara's expanding waist was much larger than the Sara in Nic's dream. The due date of their third child was only two weeks away. She nudged Nic again, then left the bedroom and shuffled back to the kitchen.

Nic moaned at the thought of the board meeting. The OSC board of directors were scheduled to gather at their home for the quarterly meeting to discuss the latest developments. Nic was not looking forward to sharing his challenges. "Michael doesn't understand what I've been going through. I doubt anybody on the board will get it either," he mumbled to himself, feeling totally defeated.

Joy is the infallible sign of the presence of God.
—Pierre Teilhard de Chardin

Although he was disappointed that only two out of the seven board members were in attendance, he was happy that the small turnout meant fewer questions and a shorter meeting. He wasn't in the mood to talk about the charity's problems.

"I know you want to hear about our latest developments." Nic spoke quickly. "We have served hundreds of families in our 'Families in Need' program. We have also provided food, medicine, clothing, furniture, and other important items to another thousand or so migrant farm worker families here in Central Florida." Nic barely took a breath between his words. "The charity now receives donated medicine and supplies that are packed for transport and can be carried by volunteers to third-world countries. Our med kits contain a variety of donated items for developing nations. They currently have a retail value of over $25,000."

"Do we pay the airfare for these volunteers?" asked a board member.

"No. Every volunteer pays all their own expenses. It costs us about $400 to package and ship materials to the volunteer and to prepare proper documents for their entry at customs. This way, nothing goes to the black market. Also, the volunteers who deliver these medicines to scheduled clinics will teach them how to use the meds that are delivered. The kit is loaded with antibiotics and vaccines that most of these areas would never be able to get."

"So OSC has done this already?"

"No, but I will leave for East Africa in two months to see how it works. I will be visiting a clinic I helped build many years ago."

"You're going to Africa?" another member asked.

"Yes, to Dandora, outside Nairobi in Kenya. I once worked with a volunteer group that built a community center there. I know it'll be the perfect place to see how this approach works."

"This is all very pretty, helping all these needy people, but what about the issue with Donna? Aren't you losing the rights to the OSC website and screenplay?"

Nic was hoping to avoid the topic. "Sara and I will pay the legal fees. She will not be a threat to us." Nic glanced at his notes, looking for the next point to focus on.

"How can you and Sara afford this?" asked the member. "You've both been paid only a couple of months of salary in all this time. And now Sara is . . ."

Suddenly, Sara called from the bedroom where she had been playing a game with the boys. "Nic! Nic! Come quick! My water just broke." The intensity in her voice was unfamiliar. "Nic, NOW!"

In a blur, Nic vacated the board meeting and rushed Sara out of the house. Once in the car, Sara focused on her breathing for the entire ride until they pulled up to the emergency room entrance. Instantly, she was in intense labor. The route to get her to the labor and delivery area seemed like an unending maze.

Sara couldn't hold in the screams as the knife of labor continued to twist in her lower back.

The staff finally got Sara into a bed. They worked anxiously around her, connecting her to an array of monitors and other devices. Sara tried to sit up to adjust her aching body, but she suddenly fainted and fell back on the cot.

"Blood pressure dropping fast," reported one of the staff. Another followed quickly, "Breathing ceased." The team rushed faster, preparing and inserting a breathing tube. Nic heard the emergency room speakers blare out, "Preparing emergency C-section."

A nursing staff member took Nic's arm. "Come with me now." She took him around the corner and helped him wash his hands. Nic dressed quickly in a surgical gown. It was all happening so fast that Nic didn't have time to think. A nurse approached and explained to him in a calm manner, "Okay sir, follow our instructions carefully. This is an intense but fast surgical procedure."

Nic turned pale. "Surgical procedure? Is Sara all right? What's happening?"

The nurse responded, still calm. "The baby's head is stuck in the birth canal. They are commencing an emergency C-section to remove the baby swiftly."

"They're going to be all right, aren't they?"

Nic didn't get an answer. He was ushered into a surgical room where Sara lay in a semi-unconscious state among the delivery equipment. Nic watched breathlessly as the staff moved through a rapid series of steps. Nic was led to sit next to Sara's head. Her arms were outstretched and strapped to boards, stuck with needles and tubes. Before Nic was a blue curtain that he could barely peer over to see the rest of her body. He stretched his neck over the curtain and watched as the doctor took handfuls of fleshy intestines out of Sara and slid them off to the side. He had to bury his arms into Sara's abdomen up to his elbows. Nic was about to faint, but a miracle happened before his eyes. The doctor suddenly pulled out a screaming newborn and held up the baby. "Here she is, everyone!"

The umbilical cord was quickly clamped and cut. The infant girl cried her protest as a nurse passed her on to others quickly. They cleaned, wiped, and wrapped the baby in seconds. The doctor looked at Nic who was standing in awe. Behind Nic's mask, his jaw was locked wide open.

"Congratulations daddy, it's a girl," yelled the doc with his hands busily rustling around Sara.

After Sara was sutured up, the staff rushed her out of the room, but Nic was held back from following.

"They must stabilize your wife now," said the head nurse. "You can't be there, but I promise you will see her soon. There's someone you have to meet first." She turned around, reaching into the small hospital crib, took the bundle into her arms, and handed him his new daughter.

Nic's spirit changed. He reached out and carefully received his daughter. Nic held her quietly and reverently, just as he did when he first held his boys. "Welcome, welcome home, Nina Maria." Nic and Sara had chosen the name in case they were to be blessed with a little girl. Suddenly Nic looked up at the nurse. "Is she . . ." Nic couldn't finish the question for fear of the answer.

"Yes," smiled the nurse. "She is alert and responded well to all initial tests. She is healthy."

Nic looked up to heaven. Closing his eyes he whispered, "Thank you, Lord Creator, thank you. Now take care of Sara for me." After a pause, while Nick felt the bliss of fatherhood, more staff entered the room. A nurse leaned over to take Nina, but Nic held on.

The doctor entered with a worried look. "Nic, I'm sorry to say your wife . . ." He stopped and swallowed hard. "Sara's in a coma. It will take some time for the anesthesia to wear off, and at that time, we can make a full evaluation. I'm sure you'll want to stay a bit before you go." He quickly exited.

"Go?" Nic yelled to the remaining staff. "I'm not going anywhere."

"I'm sorry sir," one of them said, "but we have a hospital policy. You cannot stay for more than another hour."

Nic had a tone of complete resolution. "I respect your policies. However, you will have to have me arrested to get me to leave my wife's bedside."

The staff member stepped back with a look of almost fear. "I'll see what I can do," she promised. "Soon they'll bring you to her room. Your daughter will have to go with us now."

Nic sighed and reluctantly handed over Nina. He was led into the intensive care unit. He walked into the room to see Sara connected to numerous machines. Nic quietly sat down on a chair next to Sara's bed and held her fragile hand. He looked down. Her withered arm had never felt so weak.

"Nic, be careful," cautioned a nurse. "That's her weak arm, and it has become even weaker from all the pokes to get fluids into her." The nurse gently rubbed Sara's arm. "We ran out of room on her good arm, but this one can't be of any help to us. Many of the veins are collapsing or they are just too small." She rubbed Sara's arm for a moment more. "I have to go now, but I'll be back."

Nic didn't take his eyes off of Sara's face. She looked just as she did every morning when she woke up, peaceful, content, and always very, very beautiful. Nic moved to her bedside and looked down at her as tears rolled down his face. He lowered his head to the bed. "Now, God, I need you here now, my Lord, within me and within my soulmate, Sara," he whispered.

Nic was allowed to stay with Sara for three days. But there was no change in her condition.

"Nic, it's been three days," said the doctor, who had entered the room with staff. "You promised, if there was no change by now you would go home. Your family needs to be with you. Besides, you really need a shower." Even Nic joined the staff in a small chuckle. The doctor turned to Nic. His face was drawn. "I'm not sure how much longer we can keep getting fluids into her arm. Because her weak arm collapsed, and her good arm was over-utilized, fluids are collecting, and the swelling is getting worse. Go home, Nic. I promise to call if there is any change."

Nic looked around. "Please remember to call at any time for *any* reason. Yes, I will go home for my family and a shower." He turned to Sara and leaned over to whisper, "I love you more and more each day. Don't go anywhere. I'll be right back. Blessings to you, my love. I'm off to go hold our baby girl, and will bring her here for you to see her." He kissed Sara. He allowed his mind to overtake his heart, as a dark feeling rushed over him. *Is this the last time I will ever kiss her warm lips?*

❋ ❋ ❋

NIC STRUGGLED WHILE PLAYING with the boys. What a blessing the innocence of childhood was. The boys acted as if nothing was wrong. Mommy was just at the hospital and would soon come home with their new sister. That evening, Nic sat down on the back porch while his mother put the boys to bed. He was glad his mother and father had come to Sarasota for a long stay in anticipation of the birth of their new grandchild. He stared at the candle on the table as dusk turned to dark. Tears welled in his eyes. He dropped his head on his folded arms on top of the table. "Why God?" he whispered. "Why all this? Haven't the last few years been enough? Day after day, more and more people calling in desperation for help. OSC, me, us, constantly limited with what we can do to help them. That's what this is all about, isn't it? To help and serve each other? And then what do I do? I talk Sara into letting me spend our savings, our investments, all the money we had and didn't have. We're so far in debt that we may lose our home. And now I may lose Sara. You gave us the healthy girl we prayed for, but it wasn't supposed to involve losing my wife. Why is it all falling apart? When I promised to make this vow, I figured you'd be there, that you'd always be with me and help me out when I was in need. So how can I be failing? How can so much be going so wrong?" Nic leaned back in this chair gasping for air but quickly dropped his head down again. He couldn't control his tears.

Images began to swirl in his mind, images of Sara lying in the hospital, the many different OSC struggles, their wedding day, the birth of the children. First was Pablo, the experience that changed his life forever. The moment Pablo arrived, Nic finally understood why his parents had done so much for him. This was a different kind of love, an affection of the sort that we share with the Creator, the love one feels when they experience a great gift of creation.

Then Nic reminisced about Marco. The hospital was so crowded at the full moon that poor Sara had to deliver him in the hallway in a wheelchair. They had just gotten her there on time. And then Nina. Nic revisited the excitement of her birth and the trauma of what happened to Sara. His heart sank deeper. His cries were now like low moans. He felt like he wasn't even breathing anymore, and he wasn't sure if he wanted to. In a reverie, he saw Sara's face again like he did just before he left the hospital. She was somehow so serene, so beautiful, so adorable.

With a sudden gasp, Nic sat up taking in air deeply. He began to breathe evenly again. Composing himself, he sat up tall. Nic's attention was pulled to a glowing ring that seemed to encircle their home. Bright yet shadowy figures began to become clearly visible just above the porch. Nic jumped up as he rubbed his eyes dry. They were angels, standing tall and arm-in-arm, foot next to foot. Nic kept rubbing the tears away as he focused on the one angel that was brighter than the others.

Nic's breathing stopped again. In the link of these angels was Sara smiling right at him. In a gesture of confidence, she broke the arm link with the other angels. They all directed their attention to her as she raised high her withered arm. The ring of angels began to fade and disappear, one by one from both sides of the circle. As they vanished from sight, the only figure left was Sara and her smiling face. Behind her stood a glorious angel unlike the others. Sara basked in its radiant light, which wrapped powerfully around her silhouette. Something about this special angel seemed familiar. Then the entire vision faded to a single image: Sara's withered arm, held high and glowing with the same powerful, radiant light.

Nic's phone rang loudly, scaring Nic as he gasped for air. Nic reached aggressively for the phone. "Yes," he yelled.

A monotone voice answered. "Mr. Perugino?"

"Yes," he yelled again.

"It is imperative that you come to the hospital immediately."

"What's wrong?"

"You need to come right away sir. The situation is . . ."

Nic didn't wait for the answer.

* * *

STANDING IN SARA'S ROOM, Nic was surrounded by hospital staff. Sara's doctor put his arm over Nic's shoulders as they stared at Sara together.

"Nic, there is no option here. Her good arm is too swollen and bruised from the needles and tubes we have inserted into it over the past few days while she was in the coma. We have to disconnect the tubes and wait to see how long it will take."

Nic didn't understand. "How long *what* will take?"

"This is a very unfortunate situation, Nic. Her body is too weak. This will not be easy. We have no idea how long she can last."

Nic just stared at her. He took a deep breath. "Stick her withered arm with what she needs," he commanded.

The staff exchanged glances. No one was smiling. Some had to leave the room. Sara's doctor held on to Nic's shoulders tightly. "Nic, that's just a waste of time. This is a most challenging time for us who love life and work so hard to preserve it . . "

Nic interrupted him. "Use her withered arm," he demanded. "It's her strongest arm. I know it. She carried the children with it. Use it now, I insist." He turned and looked into the doctor's eyes. The remaining staff looked at each other while grabbing what they needed to try one more time. The doctor acknowledged their readiness. Silence dominated the room. The doctor looked at Nic and then Sara and gave the nod to go ahead. They worked swiftly and with a determination rarely witnessed. Nic got pushed to the back of the room as they made calls and gave orders and signals. They checked their work and began to back away. One by one they left. Each seemed to stare at Nic as if they were saying with their eyes, “We’ve done our best. Good luck.”

Nic was finally alone. Quietly pulling up a chair, he sat and held onto Sara’s tiny hand. The entire arm was plugged with tubes and needles and strapped to a board. Sara’s face looked like she was just about to wake. He felt as if tomorrow will be another morning, and just like every morning, he would watch her awaken again.

* * *

EARLY THE NEXT MORNING, the ICU staff worked quietly at the nurses’ station after receiving a routine briefing on the previous night’s activity. A buzzer sounded. Loud snoring was heard over the speaker. The staff started to giggle. “Oh that old man Mason, there he goes again. That snore is the strongest part of him.” The nurse reached to turn down the intercom but stopped when she heard a faint voice.

“Please, please,” a weak voice begged. “Can somebody stop the noise . . . Please stop the snoring.”

The nurse started to run. “My God, it’s from Sara’s room!” she yelled, running down the hall. As the others followed, another turned up the intercom in disbelief.

“Someone pleeeeeease stop the snoring.”

The staff burst through the door to Sara’s room. Nic was slumped over in the chair, snoring loudly. Sara was smiling and looking at him. She looked up at the staff, and with the voice of a little girl said, “Can you please help me to shut him up. I’ve got a headache.”

One of the nurses stopped as the others running into the room bumped into her from behind. “Sara, this is wonderful.” The nurse’s exclamation scared Nic and he jumped, slid out of the chair, and landed on the floor. Quickly he leaned up onto his knees to look at Sara.

“What’s wrong? What’s happened?” He realized that Sara’s bright eyes were open. “Sara,” he whispered sweetly, “you’re awake.” Nic slowly stood in wonder.

Sara smiled faintly. “You know your snoring always wakes me.” She slowly reached for her stomach. “My baby. Where’s my baby?” Her face turned to panic as she stirred herself nervously.

Nic calmed her immediately. “Safe and happy nearby.”

A nurse by the door yelled, “I’ll go get her right away.” She exited quickly.

Sara leaned back on the pillow, her eyes wide. “Her? Her? Then Nina Maria is here?”

Nic started to cry. “Oh, Sara, you did it, she’s a beautiful little girl.”

The staff moved aside to make an aisle from the door to the bed. Nic and Sara turned to watch Sara’s doctor walk in with Nina. Without a word, he gently laid her next to Sara’s head. Sara tried to reach her, but her arms could only move slightly. Sara looked upset.

“My arms. I want to hold her.”

“Hold her with your gorgeous face. Your arms will be just fine. Give them some rest now,” Nic whispered as he snuggled with his wife and daughter for the first time.

The staff quietly left the room, giving the family a few minutes, all whispering in amazement over the miracle they just witnessed. Sara was fixed on Nina’s face. “Ahh, she’s as beautiful as the boys,” she whispered.

Nic nodded. "Yes, she's all her mother."

A nurse slowly entered the room. "I'm sorry, but I need to take the baby, and you will need to leave, Mr. Perugino. We need to evaluate your wife."

Nic stood slowly. He leaned over Nina and kissed her on her forehead. He looked deep into Sara's eyes. "I was afraid I was going to lose you."

Sara wrinkled her nose. "You didn't believe?" With great effort, she lifted her head slightly. "You don't get it, Nic. Great things can happen if you just believe."

"I believed. I was just afraid."

Sara lowered her head. "If you truly believe, you won't be afraid."

The nurse gently took Nina and looked at Nic.

"Yes, I'm leaving."

Sara closed her eyes. "Believe, Nic," she whispered. "I believe in you. I believe in your heart and in your spirit." Sara's voice faded as she repeated, "Believe, believe, believe."

* * *

SARA FULLY RECOVERED, and her traumatic experience soon became an unwanted memory. Her words to Nic were also quickly forgotten, leaving Nic very apprehensive about going to Africa and leaving Sara and the boys.

"You know what a big step this is for OSC," encouraged Sara as she bounced six-month-old Nina on her knee. "It's taken a long time to set up the medical kits, and now you get to deliver the first shipment."

"I know. I can't believe it," said Nic, smiling briefly. His smile quickly disappeared. "I'm going to be worried about you all. Maybe I should postpone it another few months."

"You will do no such thing. We will be taken care of, Nic."

Nic leaned towards Sara and he kissed her lovingly, prompting an unpleasant memory to flash through his mind. It was the same horrible feeling that he had when he kissed Sara the night he left her at the hospital, wondering if that kiss would be their last.

13

The most beautiful moments in life are moments when you are expressing your joy, not when you are seeking it.
—Jaggi Vasudev

Nic rode in a truck on a bumpy dirt road in Nairobi, Kenya with his old friend Tommy, and Joe, an OSC volunteer and close friend. Joe was a photographer and eager for the adventure. Nic was happy to have the excited traveling companion, knowing Joe had no idea what he was about to experience. Nic shook his head in despair. "I can't believe how it's changed so much. It seems even more overcrowded and even more neglected since my last visit."

Tommy didn't seem to notice the crowds. "It's been over sixteen years since you were here. People keep coming to town looking for work and protection from the rebels in the mountains."

The look on Joe's face portrayed the initial shock of his surroundings that Nic was very familiar with. Nic looked around. The crowds of people seemed even thicker than he remembered. Children shifted through hills of garbage on the side of the road, searching for salvageable items. *Even though there was chaos back then, there was at least some order, some sense of dignity in the crowds.* Instead of a sea of people, the crowd was more like a typhoon whose waves were crashing and stirring up havoc. Their desperation lingered in the air.

Tommy pulled the car over. "We must leave the car here and walk. The road is out up ahead. It's not much further." He pointed up the road. "Look, you can see the clinic and community center you helped build over there." He continued to point through the crowd.

Nic squinted. "It all looks so different. I never would have recognized it." Nic kept looking around for a familiar landmark. "Have the buildings been moved since they were built?"

Tommy laughed. "No. These are the same ones you helped build brick by brick."

They grabbed boxes from the trunk and stepped carefully, trying to avoid the puddles along the street.

"I thought there was a drought, so why is there so much dirty water on the street?" questioned Nic, almost losing his footing.

Tommy kept walking. "We're stepping over sewage, Nic. The sewage system installed here got overwhelmed by too many things that didn't belong in it. It fell into disrepair and is now abandoned. There's no money to repair it."

Nic scowled, stepping even more carefully.

"Watch your step, please." Tommy pulled open the canvas door of the clinic for Nic. "Go on in."

Nic and Joe ducked their heads slightly as they walked under a sheet that covered the low, narrow door. The room was packed with ailing people. Those who could stand were pacing around. Their eyes were dull. Their skin looked like dried parchment. An overwhelming odor of sickness hung heavy over the desperate crowd. Children were crying, and the elderly were sitting on the floor holding their heads in their hands. Nic's heart sank. Carrying two cameras, Joe followed behind him, ready to document every moment of their journey. Joe was stunned by the scene, yet intrigued by what he saw. He held up his camera to take a picture of an elderly man curled up on the floor in the corner of the room, his red eyes watering with pain. He focused in on the man, then lowered the camera. It didn't seem right to document his misery.

"Tommy," yelled someone suddenly. The entire mood of the room changed. Everyone stood who could. They began smiling and cheering. Some of the patients approached Tommy, reaching out to shake his hand or hug him. He calmed them down gently with a wide smile.

"*Jambo, Si-jambo.*" Tommy addressed the gathering in Kiswahili. "It is good to see you also. I want you to meet friends from the U.S. who have brought boxes of medicine for the clinic." The crowd responded in an uproar of thanks and praise.

Tommy led Nic and Joe through the crowd to the next room where another noisy crowd waited. Tommy placed his box on a low, narrow table. Nic did the same. Dr. Mike entered the room from around the corner, drying his hands.

"*Jambo*, good to see you again." Nic remembered Dr. Mike as one of the doctors staying with Tommy. Dr. Mike nodded a welcome, then turned to the table and handed Nic a small knife. "Okay, like to cut the ribbon? Tommy told me about your relief agency. This is your first medical kit delivery, right?"

"Yes. Yes it is," stuttered Nic, a little overwhelmed by the scene. He accepted the knife and turned to look through the window to the lobby full of people. There they were, *all* of them, staring at the box through the opening. They were so quiet, somehow, even the babies, that Nic froze for a moment in amazement. As he turned back to the box, he could feel each person in the lobby gazing in anticipation. "I feel as if I am about to open a priceless box of jewels," chuckled Nic.

Dr. Mike smiled. "You are."

Nic sliced through the first box. Dr. Mike pulled open the flaps and started handing supplies to the staff.

You'd think I just scored a winning touchdown, thought Nic as everyone cheered in the lobby. He handed a folder to Dr. Mike. "Here's the packing list."

Dr. Mike scanned each and every item like a child in a toy store before passing it along: penicillin, amoxicillin, oral rehydration tablets, pain killers, ointments, children's vitamins, prenatal vitamins. "Nic, this is excellent," said Dr. Mike. "And there's more available?"

Nic looked out into the lobby again. "Yes, there is, but there are so many here in the clinic. I feel like these boxes are such a small drop in the bucket that it just doesn't make a difference."

Dr. Mike froze. He put down the items in his hands and looked at Nic. "These meds will provide much relief and save many of their lives. There is nothing small about that." He resumed scanning each item and then passed the medicines out to be placed on shelves. Nic noticed that some of the staff were holding textbooks and comparing pictures to the supplies being placed on the shelf.

"For most of these health care students, this is the first time they get to see what they have been learning about," explained Tommy, sensing Nic's observation. "This is a very exciting day for them."

Joe never said a word. He was too busy snapping photos and taking videos the whole time. Children sang and danced around them as they walked back through the lobby to leave the clinic. The rest were clapping and cheering. The commotion was a bit unnerving for the guests. Just as they got to the doorway, an elderly woman jumped at Nic and grabbed onto him. She stared deeply into his eyes in a way that he had never experienced and began to yell at him in Swahili. Her sudden outburst made Nic jump, causing him to trip on his way out the door. Joe quickly leaned against Nic, catching him from falling into the sewage near the doorway.

"Thank you, Joe. Even if none of the pictures come out, you've earned your keep just now." Nic laughed as they walked down the street to the car. "That woman really scared me. What did she say?"

Tommy smiled as they settled into the car. "She said 'May God bless you abundantly.' It is a great honor to serve the poor. They are always so appreciative. We share what we have to offer, our medicine, our knowledge, and when that runs out, we offer our prayers and hearts."

They drove through the crowded streets for a short distance and stopped at a small business offering vehicle rentals. They got out of the car to say their goodbyes.

"You're really happy here Tommy, aren't you?" expressed Nic as they hugged.

Tommy stepped back and smiled. "You can't place a price on the love these people give in return for our help,"

Nic agreed, but he couldn't understand Tommy's contentment with his minimal abilities to help these people. This delivery didn't make him feel better about what he was doing as he had hoped. However, he did feel good about where they were headed to next. He felt like he needed a break.

* * *

THE RENTED LAND ROVER moved slowly through downtown Nairobi with Nic at the wheel and Joe as his passenger.

"Not many paved roads around here," Joe said as he held on tightly.

"Nice and bumpy too," laughed Nic. "In several minutes, human civilization will cease to exist."

Joe looked at Nic. "Hope that doesn't include us."

"We'll camp at the base of Kilimanjaro by dark," instructed Nic.

Joe looked worried. "What? We're camping out in the middle of the African Plains?"

Nic laughed. "I'm taking you to a place that is an oasis for the wild and the civilized. It's a very private resort at the base of Kilimanjaro. I stopped there during a break between assignments when I was here years ago. You're going to love it. It's a great place to re-energize. It's a little bit of the life we know at home but extra special because it's in the middle of all of this."

A sign at the side of the road read 'Amboseli National Park'.

"This is it." Nic turned to look behind them at the setting African sun, then turned forward again. "Mount Kilimanjaro." He pointed to a huge mass in the distance in front of them. "That's where we're going." He put the Land Rover in gear.

It was amazing how quickly the giant mountain rose in the plains as they sped towards it. Gazelle and zebra raced them in stretches. They stopped for a time as rhino meandered across the road. Joe was busy filming, finding it difficult to keep up with all of the photo opportunities.

The approaching darkness revealed a blanket of stars. They continued to follow the road towards the mountain.

"We're in the southern hemisphere here," said Nic. "You may have never seen these stars before in your-"

A sudden rumble interrupted Nic. The rumble quickly turned into a loud roar. Suddenly, their Land Rover was washed off the road by a flash flood as they were approaching a small bridge. The vehicle stalled, water seeping in under the doors.

"We're sinking!" yelled Joe in a panic "We've got to jump out!"

Nic put his hand on Joe's chest, holding him in his seat. "No, it's okay. I don't think so. The water has stopped. Get the flashlights, but don't open your door."

They both held their feet up off of the flooded floor. Joe handed Nic a flashlight and they turned them on at the same time. Joe pointed down to his feet. "My feet are soaked. There's more water on my side than on yours."

"We've stopped sinking," Nic observed. He flashed his light outside. "Looks like we're in a swamp." He pointed the light upwards over a hill. "And look, there's the bridge I was headed for. It must have been a mini flash flood off of Kilimanjaro that knocked us into this swamp. I never even saw the water."

"When are we going to get out?" Joe shook his wet feet in the air.

Nic kept looking around outside with his light. "At sunrise, Joe."

"Sunrise? You mean we have to stay here all night? Why? You said we weren't far."

"Why?" Nic answered calmly. He pointed the flashlight out of the jeep, shining the beam no more than twenty feet away. "That's why," he said soberly, "and there's more."

Joe gasped. There was a herd of hyena bouncing around, excited to see their new visitors. Joe swallowed hard. "Are there other animals out there?"

"Think about where you are," answered Nic, annoyed with the question "Nighttime is when they come out to feed."

Joe fidgeted in his seat, clearly very upset

"Stay calm," instructed Nic. "It's getting very uncomfortable in here."

"Then we open our windows," Joe said as he reached for the handle.

"No!" Nic yelled grabbing Joe's arm. "Take a look out there. There are too many bugs. They'll eat us alive." Nic reached down to the key still in the ignition. "I wonder . . ." He turned the ignition on but got no response at all. "I'm not surprised," said Nic. "The engine is half-submerged. But it looks like the battery isn't. Some lights are on."

"What will that do for us?" snarled Joe. Nic reached for the headlights. He turned them on with no luck. "Trying to signal the hippos that we're here?" snorted Joe.

Nic rolled his eyes with a sigh. "I was hoping they may work. The resort staff often look for headlights flashing high beams in the night, signaling the need to be rescued." Nic and Joe sat silently for a few moments. Their peace was disturbed by something bumping into the front of their vehicle. Joe sat up and yelled.

"We're rescued!"

"Quiet," snapped Nic. He had his flashlight fixed on two red lights right under the water. Nic turned it off and whispered, "You had to say hippo, didn't you. Stay quiet." The Land Rover jolted again.

"There's more than one," panicked Joe.

"There'll be more if you don't shut up," hushed Nic.

They didn't speak for nearly an hour. Joe finally turned to Nic. "Okay to whisper?"

"I think so," Nic whispered back without moving a muscle. "It's been quiet out there, a little too quiet. You don't see many animals now, but they come out at night, especially the big cats and other predators."

Joe swallowed hard, afraid to move. "Lions?"

"Lots, but we're inside the Land Rover and should be safe unless the baboons find us."

"What possible harm could they do compared to a lion?" asked Joe.

Nic laughed quietly. "I know it's hard to believe, but they've been known to smash windows and get into trucks."

Joe sank slowly down in his seat. "We're going to die."

Nic laughed again. "Hopefully not tonight." Pointing upward through the front window, he said, "Check out the stars. They're all so different."

"Are you nuts? There's a chance we won't see the sunrise, and you're admiring the stars?"

There was a scurry on the ground near their vehicle. The hyena ran away howling. The hippos bumped them a few more times, and then all turned eerily quiet. Nic turned on a flashlight and shined it out the window and into the eyes of a large lioness standing on the bridge, not ten feet away. She stared down at them as if a statue.

Joe knocked the flashlight out of Nic's hand. It fell into the water on the floor. "Turn it off, you're going to get us killed."

"Nice move," Nic whispered. "Now we have only one flashlight, and those were the fresh batteries too."

"But we're surrounded by lions," Joe panicked.

"Shhh, whisper," cautioned Nic. "It's a good thing they're here, now we can sleep."

Joe began hyperventilating. "Oh, that makes good sense."

"Will you please whisper?" cautioned Nic. "Now that the lions are here, it will keep the baboons away. The lions can't get us in here, remember?"

"Well, at least the headlines will make us look good," said Joe, finally whispering. "They'll read, 'They died delivering medicine to children in Africa.' I'm sure Sara and your kids will be impressed."

"Listen, Joe." Nic was ready to punch his companion unconscious to shut him up. "We have to be quiet. You're getting hysterical, and you're getting on my nerves. Just try to sleep. I'll keep watch."

With a huff, Joe turned his back to Nic and wrapped himself in a blanket. Nic didn't understand how he could stand the heat, but at least he was quiet. Nic sat back and got comfortable, staring up through the windows at the stars. After a while, he looked over at Joe all wrapped up in a blanket murmuring quietly in a restless sleep. He looked back at the stars. *Dear God, please get me out of this alive. I'm just getting started here. I still have a lot to do and so many people to help.*

A lion's roar sounded far away, but a quick check with the flashlight indicated more were right outside their Land Rover. Leaning his head on the window, he continued his conversation with the stars. "What is wrong with me?" he whispered. "I was worried about leaving Sara and the kids, but I just had to deliver that medicine. I had to prove myself. Now look at the situation I'm in. All I've proven is that I can't do this." The twinkling blanket of stars looked as if they were dancing with joy. They reminded him of the sparkle in Sara's eyes and the innocent joy in his children's hearts. "Funny thing how I spend so much energy getting people to focus on the children of the world, and I forget to focus on my own." He scowled with disappointment in himself.

14

To get the full value of joy you must have someone to divide it with.

—Mark Twain

Hours passed. Nic noticed the stars fading and saw shadows of animals moving about. The sky moved from black to midnight blue. Slowly, yet quickly, dawn arrived. It was a crystal clear dawn. The snowy-white peak of Kilimanjaro was sunlit in the distance. Thousands of pink flamingos meandered through the swamp they slept in.

The cries of a clan of hyenas rushing the flamingos abruptly awakened Joe. Stunned, his feet plunged into the water below him. "I thought we were under attack."

Nic laughed. "Not yet. Boy, you sleep soundly. Is it because your feet were in water?"

Joe looked down and saw his feet resting in the dark brown swamp water. "Ugh. What a mess. What kinds of diseases am I going to get from this water?" Joe turned his head to look at Nic. "Sorry about the attitude last night, Nic."

"No problem," Nic responded. "I was going to wake you. I want you to see the sunrise on Kilimanjaro." He pointed through the windshield. It was a most majestic sight. Clouds were swirling just under the snow-capped mouth of the volcano. The sun's rays came in shots of long shades of pinks, yellows, and pure white light. They were both in awe as the bright sun quickly descended on the volcano, sweeping across the African plains. As their eyes followed the sun's brilliance toward them, they both looked to the sides and afar. They were surrounded by thousands of pink flamingos. Nearby there were hundreds of wild animals roaming within one hundred yards from their Land Rover. Beyond them, there were thousands by the score. There were herds of elephant, gazelle, zebra, ostrich, hyena, rhino, and multitudes of birds. A hippo stared at them from the front of the Rover.

"For a moment, it was all worth it," sighed Joe. "Then I saw all of these animals. Now what do we do?"

"At least we didn't sit in water all night."

"Speak for yourself," Joe said with disgust as he shifted in his seat, revealing the puddle he slept in.

Nic jumped. "Look."

Joe huddled in the seat. "What's out there?"

"Look, there's a van. It's a safari van from the resort. Help me take the rearview mirror down. We'll use it as a reflection to get their attention."

Joe started to unscrew the mirror. Nic climbed out the window onto the hood waving his yellow shirt. Joe struggled and eventually pried the mirror off the frame, reaching it out his window to Nic. "Here's the mirror. Hurry they're turning away." Nic tried his best, but the sun was off to his side behind him. The reflection didn't work. Joe pounded the side of the Land Rover. "They can't see us," Joe complained. The pounding disturbed the hippos and they started rocking the Land Rover.

"Easy Joe," Nic yelled as he fell over, landing on the hood with a bang. "What's wrong with you?"

Joe grumbled, leaning further inside his window. "Look, another one," yelled Joe, pointing to another van. "Hurry, try the mirror. They have to see the reflection."

"No, they won't, Joe. Get up here, and wave something big and bright."

Joe was challenged with his wet shoes, but he slipped his way out the window and climbed onto the hood, stepping carefully as if he was walking on ice. A photo-safari van drove straight for them, then turned away. Joe banged his foot on the hood, causing him to slide into Nic. Nic stepped on a wet spot and slipped, feet first towards the water. As he fell, Joe grabbed his arm. Nic landed on his stomach.

"Nice catch," Nic breathed.

"There's a part of me that wants to share my wet-feet feeling with you right now," threatened Joe.

Nic smiled. "But you're too nice of a guy, Joe, right?"

Joe helped Nic up to the roof. Joe sighed with a moan. "They still can't see us. Are they blind?"

Nic also took a deep breath. "We see them because of the dust trail they leave, but they can't see us because they are looking into the massive sunrise behind us. Take a look."

Joe turned to see a brilliant, massive, orange sunrise. It was the largest he had ever seen. He felt as if he could reach out and touch its dancing rays. Herds of wildebeest, zebra, hyena, vultures, flamingos, rhino, and other wildlife were in full view. The companions stared blankly at the crowded plain before them. The beauty of the moment faded as the reality of the situation hit Joe. "We're doomed. We're stuck here where no one can see us, surrounded by the entire passenger list on Noah's ark."

Nic perked up. "Not for long. Hear it?" Pointing into the sun with one hand and shielding his eyes with the other, he started waving his shirt and yelling. Joe caught on quickly and joined him, for flying right over them was a small plane preparing for landing. Their eyes followed the plane. As the dust settled from the landing plane, they saw a small semicircle building about two miles away looking very misplaced in the middle of the vast plains. Nic cheered.

"This is our ticket out."

"How long do you think it will be before they come get us?" Joe asked with a hopeful tone.

Nic looked seriously at Joe. "They aren't coming to us. We're going to go to them."

Joe was dumbfounded.

"Think about it, Joe. We're almost out of water. The day has just begun, and it's beating hot already. We'll dehydrate if we stay here much longer."

Joe shook his head sternly.

Nic rolled his eyes and pointed to the airstrip. "That's the closest and only place we know for certain that there are people. Plus, the plane just separated many of the herds for us. We just follow the straight path the plane laid out. We have to hurry. The animals are still moving." He climbed through the window back into the Land Rover to collect supplies for the walk. Joe stayed on the hood as Nic kept handing him supplies. Joe kept eyeing their destination.

"That's miles away, Nic. With all these animals? No way. We're dead."

Nic growled with aggravation. "We definitely will be if we stay here any longer."

Joe screamed back hysterically. "There's no way we will be able to make it."

Nic kept handing him supplies. "You can stay if you want. We've got to leave now while there's still someone there. Are you with me?"

"I'm not staying alone," announced Joe.

"Okay, grab what you can. We can only take the essentials to travel light. We can come back to get our luggage." Nic did a supply check. "Okay, we have water, food, cameras, video-camera, money, passports, and air tickets. That should do us for now. We'll roll up the windows and lock the doors so our stuff might last a bit."

Joe was dismayed. "Shouldn't we leave the food so we don't tempt the game out there?"

Nic glared his answer at Joe.

"Hey," said Joe, trying to break Nic's stare, "grab the walking sticks that we brought for the Kilimanjaro climb. We might be able to use them."

"Great idea, Joe," said Nic, glad that Joe was finally thinking.

They disembarked the stranded vehicle and stepped into the swamp. The bottom of the swamp was warm and sticky. Their shoes filled instantly with the slimy ooze. They made sure the Land Rover doors and windows were closed tightly and locked before wading through to dry land. Hyena ran away noisily, and a herd of rhino on the road behind them stopped to grunt and stomp their feet at Nic and Joe. The intruders moved away slowly. Joe videotaped the scene.

"Filming will keep my mind occupied so I don't panic," decided Joe. "Look at that rhino," he exclaimed, studying it on his video screen. "It's so close."

"Joe, it's closer than you realize," whispered Nic. "Stay quiet and move slowly away from them. Follow me quietly. No sudden moves." He used his walking stick to prod the high grass. "That's the way to go," he said pointing. "Keep your bearings on that building." Joe followed.

"Why are you doing that with the stick?"

"To check for snakes and dens."

Joe's eyes widened. "Dens? Dens of what?"

"Dens of elephant droppings like this one," said Nic holding back the dry thick grass to reveal a massive pile. Joe enjoyed the filming and almost forgot the danger that he was in.

"I thought that smell was you," Joe joked. He panned his camera across the plain. He stopped suddenly. Joe's voice grew faint. "Nic, Nic, we have to stop."

"Why?" Nic followed the direction of Joe's video camera.

Not twenty-five feet away was a small clearing housing a lioness nursing her three cubs.

"Check it out," Nic whispered. Joe was trembling.

"What do you mean check it out? She's checking *us* out. We're breakfast."

"Calm down. She sees us, but she's nursing. We'll stay downwind of her if we slowly walk away from her a bit."

Joe swallowed hard. "But that takes us away from the landing strip and right into those herds of wildebeest and zebra."

"Precisely," said Nic. "Follow me. Let's play Moses."

"Play Moses. You're freaking me out. We're headed right to the middle of the two herds."

Nic started moving. "Is the lioness moving?"

Joe kept the camera on her as he slowly followed Nic. "No. She's still lying down and still staring at us. I can see her with the zoom lens."

"Good, follow quietly," whispered Nic. He guided them to an area with the least number of animals. The animals began to move apart. Separating before them with every step was each respective herd, moving to the left and right, clearing a path for them. Joe laughed quietly.

"I like playing Moses."

"Not quite there yet," whispered Nic, "but close enough. The building can't be much farther. I think I see an area for a runway." Joe kept filming. "Yes, the big clearing. Look, there's someone over there. We did it," Nic was elated. "I think we've made it."

They stepped out of the tall grassy area onto a large dirt runway. A Maasai tribesman walked out of the big aluminum hangar towards them. The Maasai waved. "*Jambo.*"

Nic waved back. "*Si Jambo.*"

"Where did you come from?" the man asked loudly. He was very surprised to see people emerge out of the tall grass surrounding the airstrip.

Joe put down the camera. Squinting, he pointed towards the blazing sun. "Out there," he explained.

The Maasai didn't blink. "How far?"

Now that they were safe, Joe was suddenly thrilled about their adventure. "Maybe two miles," he said proudly.

The Maasai hummed softly. "Three point four kilos?" He looked at Joe and Nic with his eyes wide. "You crazy. Why you walk in bush?"

"We got our Land Rover stuck in the swamp yesterday, and we spent the night there," Nic said. "We saw the plane land here. We were almost out of water so we followed it here." Nic raised his arms in praise. "Right here to this beautiful place." A herd of wildebeest trampled by, disappearing in the dust created by their movement. The Maasai hummed again.

"Dry season now, small swamp out there at closed bridge. Must be flood waters from Kilimanjaro. Look here." He pointed to the ground. "Lion tracks." Nic and Joe followed closely behind the slow-moving Maasai.

Joe squealed, realizing all of the sandy dirt around him was filled with countless paw prints, big paw prints.

"Many lion here," the Maasai calmly shared. "I work strip for twenty-six years. I never go in grass. Lion here everywhere." The reality of the danger that they were in sent panic burning through Joe.

"Save me!" Joe yelled as he ran towards the hangar. He reached the cement floor inside and fell to the ground. He was so happy not to see any more paw prints. The Maasai and Nic followed him to the hangar in a much more leisurely pace.

"Is this all for real?" Joe asked as he watched the dust blowing around in circles outside the hangar door.

Nic looked around and smiled. "I suspect the resort we're looking for is nearby."

"Which resort?" asked the Maasai. "Only two here."

"Amboseli Lodge," Nic said. The Maasai nodded.

"Yes, I will radio for you to be picked up now." The Maasai promptly headed towards a small office tucked in the corner of the hangar.

Nic stretched. "Got to love the service." Joe just glared at him.

The Maasai returned with a large walkie-talkie. He was smiling. "They will be here fifteen minutes."

Nic cheered. "Woo-hoo! We made it!"

Joe looked up at him with a snarl. "Made it where? To our graves? We almost died."

"Yes, and we didn't, Joe. We are alive," said Nic enthusiastically. "We'll soon be at a resort I discovered sixteen years ago. A veritable Garden of Eden, an oasis in the desert."

Joe straightened up and looked at Nic curiously. "No way. Out here?" He grew pale and swayed a bit, his head spinning from the events of the last twenty-four hours. He decided to sit back down while he waited for their ride.

The Maasai pointed to a dust cloud approaching. A van drove up to take them to their stranded Land Rover in the swamp. As they approached their abandoned vehicle, Nic yelled. "This is it. Let's get our stuff and go. I'm starved."

Returning to the accident, the situation looked almost comical. The water had subsided, and the Land Rover was buried on an angle in the thick mud. Joe jumped out of their rescue van first and, with the keys in hand, crawled through the mud to the half-buried vehicle. He started tossing their luggage and bags up onto the dry ridge as Nic retrieved them and loaded them one by one into their rescue van. Finally, they were on their way to the lodge, driving through open plains, dodging elephant, cheetah, and rhino. They passed through a forest with baboon and past a lioness kill of a wildebeest. It was a pleasure to see the animals from such a close but safe venue.

Nic looked out across the plains, thinking about the last shipment of medicine that he delivered many years ago, wondering if it really made a difference. He laid his head back on his seat, closed his eyes and thought of his archangel companion. *It's been 16 years since that night when you first told me that the answer to the world's problems was social sustainability. Nothing seems to have changed. Where is the help that you promised me, Michael? I've been waiting for that help.*

He sat still for a few moments, listening for an answer. All he heard was the squeaking and rattling of the van as it rode roughly over the terrain. Nic opened his eyes and glanced at his friend who was mesmerized by the scene outside his window.

That box of medicine that we brought to the clinic sure wasn't the answer, he thought as he frowned. Sitting up straight, he looked out his window. He decided not to think about it. *For the next few days, I'll pretend that none of these problems exist. It's much easier to just ignore it all.*

He smiled as he thought about his resort destination. If only ignoring it would make all of the problems go away. *I would be much better at ignoring it than I am at doing something about it*, Nic thought, chuckling to himself.

15

A flower blossoms for its own joy.
—Oscar Wilde

Amboseli Lodge was a resort located on an oasis nestled at the base of mighty Kilimanjaro and adjacent to Amboseli National Park, a 200-square mile nature preserve that was home to over 200 species of rare birds and wildlife. The park itself was also the home of the Maasai tribe, many of whom were part of the lodge's staff.

As they entered the resort, Nic smiled with recognition. The place was just as grand and beautiful as he remembered. The neatly kept grounds were decorated with lush greenery. Trimmed hedges wound around the property, forming a natural border and guiding guests along winding sidewalks between the buildings. Although the landscaping had been carefully planned, the grounds still had a natural beauty with an abundance of native vegetation. The buildings were styled after neighboring Maasai dwellings, their exteriors covered with red cement fashioned to resemble the Maasai mud huts and their roofs covered with tall dark grass reminiscent of the Maasai tradition of grass-thatched roofs. Wooden-plank walkways edged with banisters of wood or thick rope alternated with cement sidewalks throughout the resort.

The view from anywhere was breathtaking. The vast open plains seemed to disappear as if falling off the edge of the earth. Everywhere you looked there were wild animals; the intrusion of the busy resort did not seem to interrupt their routine. In the distance rose the daunting snow-capped peak of Mount Kilimanjaro.

As Nic and Joe disembarked from the van, an exotic-looking young woman approached to greet them, carrying a tray with two brightly colored tropical drinks. She was a Maasai, dressed in a tightly wrapped thin orange robe. She spoke very slowly, her voice adding to her mysterious demeanor.

"*Jambo*. Welcome to beautiful Amboseli Resort," she purred, offering her guests the cool beverages. Nic and Joe happily took the long-awaited refreshments with a big smile and a bow. Their hostess returned both and stepped back towards the building.

Joe couldn't help but stare at the large holes in her long earlobes. Her earrings had several stones on each, weighing them down, adding to the elongation of the flesh and skin. "Why is she wearing those weighted earrings when her earlobes are already so stretched? The holes must be three inches long," Joe asked Nic quietly, still staring at the unusual woman.

"The length of their earlobes is a sign of beauty for the Maasai women. She is considered extremely beautiful and is greatly admired here because she has very long earlobes."

"Looks painful," said Joe as he sipped on his drink.

Nic tipped his glass towards Joe's, clinking them together softly. "Happy birthday, Joe," he announced with a big smile.

Joe's jaw dropped. "What?"

"We are here to celebrate your birthday, and it will be one that you'll never forget." Nic gave Joe a friendly slap on his back.

The woman watched them intently. Nic showed her his backpack and bowed to her. She returned the bow and signaled to the staff to carry their luggage as she showed them to their room.

"You're right, this is definitely a birthday that I won't forget." Joe threw himself on the luxurious bed. "Thank you, Nic."

"The celebration hasn't even begun. I suggest we start it off with a shower and a nap."

Joe gave him a thumbs-up in agreement.

* * *

A KNOCK ON the door awakened Nic and Joe. Their Maasai hostess had come to escort them to dinner. They followed her through the lounge to the patio that ran the entire circumference of the main building, allowing a guest to sit anywhere and enjoy the breathtaking view. The sun had set, but the bright lights of the multitude of torches lit their path to a clearing where canopies had been tied onto the thin trunks of the trees, stretching over the dinner tables to protect them from seeds, sticks, and other objects falling from the trees. On one side of the dining tables was a long bar that looked like a stone wall. On the other side was a similar structure where the dinner was prepared. The chef worked fluently, flipping shrimp in a pan over the open fire. His white apron stood out starkly against the lush greens, his tall, crisp chef's hat balanced firmly on his head as he worked. He placed his finished creations on a table next to him to be retrieved by the waiters and served freshly prepared to the many guests who were still being seated.

On the other side of the clearing was a large bonfire. Chairs were set up around the fire facing the bushes, which were rustling with wildlife. Joe looked at Nic. "What are we doing here in this expensive restaurant?"

"Celebrating your birthday, what else?"

A waiter turned toward Nic and Joe, bringing a finger to his lips. "Your table is here, Mr. Joe and Mr. Nic. Please whisper."

They were seated at a table near the edge of the canopied clearing. Another waiter promptly arrived, placing the chef's hot appetizer of coconut shrimp on each plate. Nic turned and whispered to the waiter. "Thank you, sir. Just as I requested."

The hostess captivated the dinner crowd with her presence as she walked among the tables and introduced herself to the guests. Holding a torch, she quietly began. "*Jambo.* I am your hostess, Marya. Welcome and prepare yourselves to taste the flavors of Africa. Please know that whispering is requested of you during your meal, which makes it easier to lure the wildlife towards us. An hour ago, we were visited by a lion pride. They are still here. In a few moments we will turn on the spotlights and you will see them. Please do not move or make any sound. Keep cameras off until we turn on the lights."

The crowd sat quietly in the dark, looking around uneasily. Only a flimsy fence of thin fish line separated the visitors from the rustling and grunts of the wild residents. Looking out into the bushes and grassland, it was very difficult to see in the dark; it felt like there was nothing there. Suddenly, beams of soft yellow light surrounded the perimeter of the canopy.

The sight was an animal lover's dream. Elephants enjoyed a feast of their own, chewing on large mouthfuls of grass and leaves. Meandering among them was a small herd of zebra, their white stripes glowing in the spotlight. Giraffe galloped by; five adult elephants had gathered around a much smaller calf, seemingly lining themselves up in a half-circle and facing the dinner guests.

Joe tried to hold his video camera still, but his excitement made it hard for him to keep from shaking.

"They are so close. You would think that I am using the zoom lens on my camera," Joe babbled excitedly, "but I'm not."

"Look at those elephants," pointed out Nic. "It's like they are looking back at us and saying to each other, 'Look at those silly humans. Take a picture, honey.'" Joe laughed. But his laughter was suddenly squelched as another spotlight revealed yet another resident of the plains. Lounging fifteen feet from Nic and Joe's table was an old royal lion and three lionesses. Numerous cubs were frolicking in the grass.

The dinner crowd gasped as the pride caught their eye. Somehow they remained quiet and motionless. Joe squirmed.

"This will be my last birthday."

The waiter cautioned, "Shhh, be still."

The hostess continued calmly, "Soon waiters will be able to move about to serve you. Stay still and relax. This pride has been visiting us for quite some time and will move off shortly."

The royal lion jumped up abruptly and roared towards Joe. He froze. Two staff members leaped toward Joe and quickly placed themselves between him and the lion, holding rifles in position. Marya calmed the guests and cautioned them to remain still and quiet. The lion pride slowly stood up one by one and moved away, calmly roaring in unison.

Joe looked wide-eyed at Nic. It was hard for Nic to tell if Joe was scared, excited, or angry. "That was awesome," Joe finally expressed.

The dinner crowd began to chat excitably, enjoying their salad of mixed greens, fruit, and nuts. Marya continued.

"For your dinner entertainment, we have members of the local Maasai tribe to sing and dance for you."

With a wave of her hand, Maasai men and women appeared out of the darkness. They formed two lines, men in the back and women in the front. The women were wearing white robes with one wide green stripe just below the waist. Around their necks were colorful stiff bead collars that sat loosely on their shoulders and teetered up and down as they gracefully bent their knees to the rhythm. They each held a long wooden stick, grasping it with both hands and holding it upright in front of them.

"Welcome to the African story of creation," the hostess explained, gesturing to the dancers. The men began to chant and sing. They were wrapped in faded red and orange plaid, their heads adorned with a variety of headpieces. The lead entertainer sported an impressive feathered headpiece while the others wore a simple headband edged with beads. A man standing behind this line began to sing the story while the others chanted methodically. Marya glided slowly through the crowd, narrating to the enthralled dinner guests.

"When God created people, he undercooked the first batch, and so he placed them in the north. The second batch, he overcooked and placed them in the south. The third batch was perfectly golden brown. He placed them in the middle of Africa."

After each verse, the men paused as the women interjected a high-pitched loud chorus as they traveled from table to table. A plate with a large fresh swordfish filet, caught off the coast of Mombasa that morning and perfectly grilled, was placed before Nic and Joe.

"Now enjoy a meal like no other," said Nic. The colorful vegetables of string beans and squash were also very fresh, grown nearby and picked that morning. They were delicately steamed and seasoned with a tantalizing spice. Joe had never tasted a fish with such mouthwatering flavor. Meanwhile, throughout their dinner, the herd of elephants grew in number before them.

"Word must have gotten around that this is a great place to eat," joked Joe.

For dessert, they were served a variety of fresh fruit mounded on top of a light sponge cake smothered in bourbon and served flaming. It was accompanied by a rich fudge sauce for dipping. Joe leaned back, savoring his last bite. "It's hard to believe that I just finished the best meal of my life in a part of the world where so many people are starving."

Nic smiled, thinking fondly of his old friend Raja. "You can always find hope in the middle of hopelessness."

After their pleasing meal, Nic and Joe slowly walked the path back to their room and noticed a crowd near their hut. A herd of elephants were eating the plants nearby and were making noise in the darkness. Nic and Joe sat down at a table adjacent to the scene and watched as the herd slowly ate their way towards them, stopping less than fifteen feet away. A baby elephant wandered even closer.

Nic ordered two ice teas. "The Garden of Eden." He paused closing his eyes. "In the middle of so much human misery."

Joe kept staring at the elephants. "I must admit, I prefer this Africa to what we saw in Dandora and Nairobi. I never realized humans live like that. The homeless in the States have it better than the people here."

"And here they even have it good, compared to much of the rest of the world. Do you know that about two-thirds of the people in the world do not have proper sanitation and have never touched a piece of toilet paper?"

For the first time, Joe's eyes left the elephants. "No way. What kind of a world do we live in?"

Nic looked at him with empathy. "Well, our 'global village' isn't very rosy." Nic picked up his backpack and shuffled through it. "I always keep this card with me. I used to conduct high school assemblies on the world's dismal rate of poverty with the help of student volunteers." Nic handed Joe the card. Joe held it up, trying to focus on it in the glow of the torchlights. He began to read it out loud.

"If we could reduce the world's population to a village of one hundred people, the village would have sixty Asians, fourteen Africans, twelve Europeans, eight Latin Americans, five Americans, and one person from the South Pacific. The numbers would look like this:

- 52 male, 48 female
- 80 live on less than $10 a day
- 80 would live in substandard housing, no plumbing
- 70 would be illiterate
- 50 would suffer from malnutrition
- 75 without safe drinking water
- 1 has a college degree."

Joe handed the card back to Nic. "That's incredible."

Nic held up the tattered card. "If I had handed you this card just a few years ago, it would have read differently. The numbers are always changing."

"So something is being done for those in need," encouraged Joe.

Nic sighed, looking at the card in his hand. "Not enough. Think about it Joe, globally 33% of food is wasted. If each person does a small amount, then so many would not have to suffer so much." Nic sat quietly, his eyes fixed on the statistics on the card. *Ignoring it won't change anything.* He raised his head and looked around at his beautiful surroundings. *This isn't reality. I thought taking a break from it all might make it go away.*

"It isn't going to just go away," Nic mumbled to himself.

Joe could see Nic disappearing into a fog of thought. "What's the schedule for tomorrow?" he asked as a diversion.

Nic sat up, taking a deep breath. He blinked a few times, coming back to reality. "We have two safaris scheduled. Then we'll take a sunset plane to Nairobi to head back to the States. Such a short trip."

"Short? I feel as though I've lived a lifetime here."

As they boarded their airport van the following evening, Nic took one more look around before closing the door. "Someday I will bring Sara and the kids here. Then this place will really be paradise."

Their flight departed, soaring into a magnificent sunset over Kilimanjaro.

"Look Joe, it's still there. Get a picture." Nic pointed down at their stranded Land Rover just below them.

"I can't believe it's still there," said Joe fumbling for his camera. He finally positioned his camera and took a picture that would forever remind him of the most terrifying yet exciting experience of his life.

Nic looked down at the abandoned vehicle. To Nic, it symbolized something different. It looked alone and forgotten. He thought about delivering the medicine to the clinic just a few days earlier and the desperate faces of the people there. "You are not alone. I won't forget you," whispered Nic as the vast African savannah slowly disappeared from view.

16

If you can't find joy in the path you are on
and what you are working toward now,
how do you expect to find joy once you get there?
—Anonymous

Nic worked to keep true to his word, his recent travels leaving him even more passionate about making a meaningful dent in the misery he had just witnessed. He spent the next few weeks focused on the OSC board of directors, as it was time to make plans for the future. Nic gathered his five board members around the dining room table for a serious meeting. For the first time in quite a while, Nic was looking forward to the discussion and was proud of what he had to share.

"We have just delivered more than $30,000 worth of medicine in the form of our first medical kit, which cost OSC less than $400. The kit had 750 treatments including antibiotics for pneumonia and treatments for malaria, dehydration, and fever. After the success of this pilot project, OSC is now in a position to supply many more medical kits designed for developing communities." Nic paused as if he was waiting for applause.

"Nice work," said Sean dryly, "but we need to bring in many more donations if we are to keep the supplies flowing. Any ideas anyone?"

Another member, Thomas, looked over the OSC financial report. “You’re right, but first, if you don’t mind Nic, we need to pay for these expenses.” Thomas held a sheet of paper donning a long list of numbers. “What are all of these expenses in California from?”

Nic frowned. “I remember sending an email update to you all about it. Perhaps you didn’t receive it. I’m sorry to tell you that one of our volunteers flew her boyfriend and herself out to Los Angeles and went shopping on OSC’s credit card. She said she intended to pay us back but hasn’t yet.”

Thomas looked at Nic in disbelief. “You need to be more responsible, Nic. You can’t just hand the charity’s card to anyone.”

“What are all these attorney expenses?” asked the newest board member.

Nic, who had already accounted for this expenditure in an earlier email, sighed with frustration. *Nobody’s even bothering to read them*. He pointed to the memo. “OSC had a volunteer claim she owned the rights to our logo, name, and website. I had to protect OSC against this threat with multiple filings. Obviously they were expensive. I paid $3,500 of it out of my own pocket, see?” He shook a copy of the memo in the air.

“Very noble Nic,” said Sean, “but why didn’t you tell us what was going on? We could have helped.”

Thomas sat back and crossed his arms. “Nic, I’m beginning to question your ability to run this agency.”

Nic felt surprised by this blunt pronouncement. “Each and every one of you knows that I have been keeping you updated, asking for your advice and help. I understand that you are all very busy but . . .”

Thomas interrupted again. “Nic, we don’t doubt your passion to help others in need and all you have sacrificed to get here, but please realize that you've got to get a handle on running this organization. Looks to me like it's too much for one person to direct relief, fundraise, and administrate all at the same time. Why don't we all adjourn and sleep on this. I'm sure we'll find a way to work this all out."

Sean stood. "I second that. I have more productive projects to spend my time with. Good night, everyone. Goodbye, Nic." Sean and Thomas got up to leave and the rest of the group followed. Although the room was far from full with the sparse number of board members, their sudden absence left Nic feeling very alone. He turned and looked at the OSC office. It was set up in the corner of his living room, the only space available for a computer desk and file cabinets.

"What a poor excuse for an office," he muttered. "Maybe they're right."

* * *

CHRISTMAS APPROACHED AND, with Sara's encouragement, Nic continued to work on OSC. Sara finished writing the last check, closing the checkbook and giving it a pat to announce her completion. The OSC checking account was low, but she was happy that she was able to pay all of the requests for help by so many people.

"So what's the Santa schedule this year?" she asked Nic. "Make sure you don't overbook like you did last year."

"There is no schedule," he mumbled.

Sara's eyes opened wide. "What do you mean? You're usually getting quite a few requests by this time each year. I wonder what's wrong?"

"The requests have been coming," growled Nic. "But I'm just not up to wearing the suit anymore."

Sara couldn't believe her ears. "No more Santa? You? No way."

Nic turned to her, agitated. "Nothing seems to be working. I feel like I've lost the spirit to do this anymore. People are more interested in whether or not some Santa will show up to their party than they are in collecting gifts or money for people who truly need it. That's not what this holiday is about."

Sara nodded. "I see it too, especially at the stores. There's insanity in all this gift giving."

"It's more about gift *getting*," said Nic. "Christmas is nothing but a marketing joke. It's downright obscene." He turned his chair away from his desk to face Sara. "Every year around my birthday, my mom took me to the department store to have my picture taken with Santa. The day we went downtown for the photo when I was nine years old is when I really started to realize how commercialized Santa Claus had become." He became animated as he described how his mother practically dragged him down the busy downtown sidewalk, hurrying for their appointment with Santa Claus. "We had to miss our first photo appointment because I had detention after school for fighting."

Sara's eyes widened. "You? Fighting?"

"Well, not really," confessed Nic. "Kids would tease me and push me around because I believed in Santa Claus. The teachers always blamed me, saying my insisting that Santa Claus is real started the commotion."

Sara smiled at her memory of young Nic.

"That day the snow was falling as we passed store after store displaying a variety of Santas. There were Santas in front of displays, Santas holding signs, Santas ringing bells." Nic stood and slowly paced around the room as he flashed back to the scene of his childhood memory. . .

"I still can't believe you made us miss the photo shoot last week because of your detention at school. You know how important this is for you to get done every year," huffed Nic's mother.

"I'm so sorry, Mamma. I didn't mean to do it," nine-year-old Nic quietly said, holding his head down in remorse.

Together, they abruptly took a sharp turn into the oldest and largest of the department stores, pushing their way through the revolving door. Somehow, Nic's coat hood got caught in the door.

"What else can go wrong?" questioned Mamma under her breath as she stopped and pulled him free, feeling the glares of impatient disapproval from the small crowd trying to push their way through the door. Finally free, Mamma and Nic rushed up to the elevator and entered, coming face-to-face with an elderly attendant.

"Late for your appointment are you? Everyone is late today. It's a zoo up there."

"We're only thirty minutes late," panted Mamma. "Do you think we're too late?" She rested on the elevator wall to catch her breath.

"The people in line have been waiting for over an hour." The attendant yawned and checked his watch.

Mamma's breath and voice returned as she panicked. "An hour. We can't wait that long. I have dinner to get ready with all of the family coming."

The elevator door opened and more mothers with kids streamed up to the attendant. Mamma barely heard their name being blasted over the loudspeaker.

"Nic Perugino . . . is the Perugino family here?"

"Here we are," yelled Mamma, waving her hands in the air. She took a firm hold of Nic's hand and rushed him through the crowd to the front of the line. With the noisy crowd now behind him, Nic could see what everyone was so excited about. He turned to see a Santa surrounded by festive decorations, bright packages, elves dressed in red and green, and candy canes everywhere. One of the elves gently took Nic by the hand and led him to Santa who was perched on a chair fit for a king. The elf motioned to Nic to climb onto Santa's lap.

After Nic settled in, Santa looked intently upon his face. "So you must be Nic. What would you like for Christmas this year?"

Nic looked seriously into Santa's face. "I'd like to know if I can ask for something for somebody else."

"Well, I don't hear that too often, but of course you can, and what might that be?"

"Mamma made food for the homeless man that lives by the railroad tracks. He told me that he didn't have a family. Will you get him a family, you know, someone to take care of him and love him?"

Santa paused. "What a wonderful thing to ask for. I'll have to check with the elves to see if we can arrange that. That's a tall order these days. And what about the homeless man's little friend named Nic? What would he like to have?"

"Well, there is this really great Matchbox racetrack that all my cars could race on." Nic's voice rose with excitement just thinking about the possibility.

Santa looked at Mamma and got her nod of approval. "Now that's something I think we can arrange."

A nearby elf interrupted.

"Okay Nic. It's almost time for Santa to take a break. Look at the camera and smile for your picture."

Nic contentedly leaned against the Santa. His velvety soft red coat and fluffy beard felt better than Nic's own comfortable bed. The camera flashed quickly. The elf handed Mamma a slip of paper.

"Take this claim slip to customer service tomorrow to claim your photo," she instructed with a smile. Mamma took the slip of paper, holding it softly as if it were made of glass.

"We did it," she whispered as she smiled to herself. She took her billfold out of her purse, folded the claim slip, and tucked it neatly into the open pouch. She paused for a moment, her eye catching a snapshot in her wallet that was tucked behind a window of scratched plastic. A small smile curled her lips. A much younger Nic sat snuggly on Santa's lap. For a moment, her mind flashed back to the eight previous years of pictures that she had collected of Nic sitting on a Santa's lap. "He's growing too quickly," she frowned and returned the billfold carefully to her purse.

As Nic was escorted off of Santa's lap, another Santa abruptly appeared from behind the scenery. "Why are you still here?" he said angrily at the other Santa in front of the astonished crowd.

The mothers in the store cried out in shock and some shielded their children's eyes. The first Santa stood up from his throne in indignation. "Me? Why didn't *you* wait until I got back there and out of sight like you're supposed to? We both can't be out here in front of the children."

The replacement Santa snarled. "My shift starts promptly at four. You're running late. You aren't supposed to still be here."

As the two Santas continued bickering, the crowd began to scatter while some of the mothers stopped to complain to the store manager, demanding to know why their upset children had just been exposed to two Santas.

Mamma once again grabbed Nic by the hand and started her escape. She had her picture; her business was done. The distraught crowd was pushing towards the elevator, and Mamma knew it would take up too much precious time waiting their turn to complain. They quickly slipped away to a nearby staircase and ran down and out into the busy street.

"We were both out of breath when we got to the car," recalled Nic as he popped back into the living room with Sara.

He sat back down in his desk chair, exhausted from the thought of the episode. "As I got in the car and we drove away, I kept noticing all the Santas on the streets and in the storefronts. I thought about the crowd clamoring for their picture, the Santa Claus mix-up at the department store, and the commotion that it all caused. But I didn't dare bring up what I wanted to discuss."

"What was that?" Sara asked gently.

"If Santa Claus was truly real, and if he was, who was he? Was he the commercial Santa Claus that had everybody so uptight, or was he the gentle caring soul that I felt that he was?"

Sara walked over to Nic and sat down on his lap. She wrapped her arms around him and gently said in his ear, "You are living proof that his spirit is real."

Nic returned the embrace. His eyes widened with surprise. "That's exactly what my mom said to me that night," said Nic as he sat back. Looking into Sara's eyes he caught a glimmer of blue, red and green sparkles.

"Is it? Well, your mother was right." Sara stood and playfully tussled his hair with her fingers.

"The idea of Santa Claus comes from the giving spirit of Saint Nicholas, not from the selfish spirit of society," Nic grumbled, jerking his head away from Sara's touch.

"What if you dress up as Nicholas instead of Santa? It could be a statement against all the commercialism. You can teach children about charity and sharing and . . ."

The phone rang. Nic answered. "Hello, this is OSC." The caller on the other end seemed frantic.

"Can you help me? I need some help. We are getting evicted today, and I have no place for my children. We need help. I understand you pay rent for people getting evicted."

Nic closed his eyes. "Yes, we usually do, however I'm very, very sorry to say we do not have any funding available right now to help." He could hear the woman sobbing.

"But what am I going to do? I've called the other agencies. No one will help. They all told me to call you. You're the last one."

Nic kept his eyes closed as tears started to well. "I'm sorry Ma'am, there's nothing I can do. I wish there was a way to help."

"Doesn't anyone care? I'm going to lose my home. I have two young children. Where can we go?" She abruptly hung up on Nic.

He turned to Sara. "What am I to do? I can't help anybody. Not with $54.45 left in our account." He dropped his head. "All spent. We had all those surprise expenses from the incidents with volunteers. We sent medical kits to several countries, and we've been helping out more families than usual. You know how it is this time of year. More people are out of work, more are homeless and desperate during the holidays. And what can we do? Nothing."

"You *are* helping Nic."

"Not enough."

"What does enough mean to you?" challenged Sara. "When will it *be* enough?"

Nic shook his head, avoiding an answer. "You've been great, Sara. You've been behind me all this time. I've used up our savings, retirement accounts, investments, college funds. I've over mortgaged the house and we've been living on credit cards. I've ruined everything."

"Our lives are not ruined," Sara insisted. "Our lives are better because of all the help we've provided."

Nic looked defeated, despite her encouraging words. "I'm so frustrated with the whole thing. All those empty promises by so many. If we would have received ten percent of what we were promised, just ten percent, it would be a success."

Sara raised her voice slightly to gain Nic's attention. "You didn't answer me. When will it be enough?"

Nic got up and began to pace, once again avoiding Sara's questions. "We have to file bankruptcy next month," Nic moaned. "Without an income, we're going to lose our home."

"Nic, stop it," scolded Sara.

Nic stood still. Sara's tone finally caught his attention.

"Stop feeling sorry for yourself, stop blaming everyone and everything else, and stop saying you haven't done anything." Now Sara was the one pacing while Nic stood frozen. He felt like a child being lectured by a parent. "You are putting your trust and faith in the wrong places. You think you are a failure. Your only failure is your failure to believe in the spirit inside you and what it can do." Sara stopped pacing and stood in front of Nic. "You don't get it."

"What don't I get?" Nic blurted. He was getting tired of hearing this accusation.

She placed her hand gently on his chest. "Great things can happen if we just believe."

"You're right. I don't get it. I don't get why you believe in *me*," proclaimed Nic, throwing his hands up in the air. "I don't get how you can so calmly support me and encourage me through every frustration and disappointment. You're the only one helping me. In fact, if it wasn't for you, I would have quit a long time ago."

As the words passed through his lips, Nic remembered Michael's promise to send him help. *Where is all of the help that Michael promised? In fact, Michael hasn't even been helping me. Where has he been?*

Nic stepped back from Sara mumbling, "He's even given up on me."

"Who has given up on you?" asked Sara.

Nic did not respond, standing still with his head hung low.

Joy is the holy fire that keeps our purpose warm and our intelligence aglow.
—Helen Keller

"You need to get some rest," said Sara gently. She reached for Nic's hand and held it firmly. "Come on. It's time to get some sleep." She started to pull Nic away.

Nic laughed. "Sleep? Are you kidding? I can't rest with all this on my mind." He walked to the lanai and stepped outside into the refreshing evening air. He turned around to Sara who was following him. "I'll go to bed soon. I have to pray about this." He sweetly kissed Sara's cheek.

"Don't make it too late," instructed Sara. "Things will get much clearer if you don't skip sleep."

Nic walked out to the lanai. Staring up at the stars, he began conversing with them.

"Well, here we go again, and I have no idea what to do. I really need some help, Lord. I really do. I don't know where to go with this anymore. I've done my best. I've tried everything. If you really want this, you've got to help me out. You have to send somebody to help me out."

Nic felt a strange yet familiar sensation around him. Turning in circles he asked, "Michael? Where are you?" As Nic turned, he bumped right into Michael. "You're here!" yelled Nic with relief as he stretched his arms wide to give him a big hug. Michael looked at him, returning the embrace.

"I'm always with you Nic. Haven't you realized that yet?"

"Michael, I'm really in trouble. I have no income, all of my credit card and bank debt is at the limit, and all of my retirement savings are gone. Am I just a fool? I've hit bottom financially."

Michael laughed. "From where I stand, I don't know a human who isn't foolish, at least during a few times in their life." He strolled in a circle around Nic. "Still complaining, I see."

Nic bombarded Michael with his frustration. "Where have you been? I thought you'd given up on me. I need help. Are you here to finally help me? What's taken you so long?"

Michael stopped walking, his back turned to Nic. "Nic, I am here to tell you of something important about to happen at this time when you are facing great challenges. This is the night you will become more aware of the divine spirit dwelling inside of you. And you will also be visited by three angels—very important ones."

"The ones Nicholas said were coming?"

Michael nodded. "Yes."

Nic planted his fists on his hips. "Well, it's about time." Michael stopped him.

"They've been here for quite some time."

"Well, where have they been?" demanded Nic impatiently.

Michael smiled with a look of fatherly care. "They've been waiting for you to prove your commitment to the vow."

Nic raised his eyebrows. "How? By jeopardizing my family's future and well-being? By being a financially irresponsible fool?"

Michael looked sternly at Nic. "Remember, you have free will. If that's how you want to look at it, you can make that choice.

I can only see the right way to look at it." Michael stepped closer to him. "Nic, listen to the voice of the spirit within you and put aside the distractions of this world. *All* things are possible for God. For their part, humans must practice the cardinal virtues of hope, generosity, and courage."

Nic's blank stare matched the feeling in his mind. "Generosity is the part I don't get. Why has so much gone wrong? Why so many empty promises? Why so many failed attempts at raising money to help so many suffering people? I've lost so much money. It really feels as if I shouldn't be in the charity business at all. It's so hard to keep hoping with so much failure all around me." Nic waited for answers. "Michael?" Nic looked around. Michael had vanished. "That's it? Thanks a lot!" he yelled to the air around him. "Just when I thought you were here to help me out." Nic looked up at the stars again. "Is any of this ever going to make sense and work out?" He dropped his head with a loud sigh, shuffled inside, and went to bed.

Nic was restless that night, tossing and turning and moaning. His tossing landed him in a position facing the window. Waking himself with a snore, his eyes opened. Nic saw an intense red glow coming toward him from through the window. The entire wall began to glow a vibrant red with shades of orange dancing among the intense glimmerings of color. The glow shot out beams of light, which crossed each other, filling each corner of the bedroom. Nic jumped up out of bed, eyes wide.

"FIRE! FIRE! SARA! THE CHILDREN!" Nic leaned over the bed to wake Sara, pushing on her back. He collapsed over the bed as his hands moved right through her transparent body. He jumped to his feet and stepped back slowly as he realized that he was looking down at himself lying on the bed. The red glow grew with more intensity in the room. Nic turned to the wall and saw it engulfed in flames. He stood motionless.

Oh my God. I'm dead!

The sound of a roaring fire intensified, but it gave out very little heat. As the rolling flames licked Nic's body, he felt a pleasant warmth. The tongues of fire swirled until the outline of a figure appeared before him. The face of a majestic female figure slowly came into view, followed by the image of her heavenly body. Her fiery being radiated its glow in all directions. She began to speak to Nic.

"No, Nic, you're not dead, and neither is your family." Her voice was a crisp, sizzling whisper.

"Then I'm about to be?" he asked, looking around for an exit from the inferno.

"The human body starts dying the day you are born," she said. "But who you are does not." She stepped closer to Nic. Raising her arms she announced, "I am LorEl, the Spirit of Fire and the Angel of Hope. I am here to teach you lessons from the light of God. You will come with me now. Step into my being so I can take you on a journey."

She held out her hand, reaching for Nic to accompany her. Trembling, Nic glanced over at Sara, sleeping comfortably amidst the conflagration. Nic turned back to the angel. *She is one of the angels that Michael said would be coming to help me. I have to go with her.* Hesitating, he stepped forward and cowered as the flames encompassed him.

Nic stood before a chaotic crowd in familiar surroundings. "I've been here before," he blurted. "This reminds me of the Gomoh Train Station in India. But it's so different that it can't be."

LorEl pointed to a sign that said "Gomoh" and spoke firmly, "It is indeed."

Nic was awestruck as he looked at the flourishing city before him.

"Come," motioned LorEl. She was still engulfed in flames, but the intensity had diminished.

They walked along the road leading to the old leper school. He marveled as he observed everyday people shopping in modern stores in well-constructed buildings. Patrons were enjoying meals in pleasant outdoor restaurants. *There aren't any beggars*, he thought as he walked along the clean streets. His pace slowed. "It can't be," Nic muttered to himself as they reached the top of a small hill and approached the school. The only familiar sight was the happy faces of children running around the compound. But these children were clean and dressed in nice clothing. "They're all wearing shoes," Nic observed as he walked across the courtyard. Modern buildings surrounded him, with stylish lights that lit up their entranceways. Nic turned to the angel at his side. "They even have electricity."

LorEl stepped up to a building and peered into the window. "Come, Nic," she instructed, making room for him next to her.

Nic peered into the window at the rows of neatly arranged beds and dressers in the dormitory. Nic shook his head in disbelief as he remembered his shock when he first learned that the children slept on the ground. "This is nothing like it was when I was here." Nic looked around, still amazed. An outdoor cafeteria donned modern equipment and sinks with running water, offering a variety of fresh, cooked foods. *I only had rice to eat*, remembered Nic with a frown. "How did all of this happen?"

"You did this. This is the result of your hope," said LorEl. "Inspired by the Spirit, several devoted volunteers came to this place and offered hope for a better future. Thanks to a lot of hard work under their leadership, the staff, and the volunteers started a movement of reform at this school that eventually changed this part of India. Wealthy philanthropists from India's high-tech sector stepped forward and donated millions. Leaders arose who overturned the corruption in local government. The school graduated so many educated and rehabilitated lepers that they ended up teaching the whole region to work together for the common good."

Nic and LorEl began to hover, looking at the town from above. "Everything has changed. The feeling of desperation is gone," whispered Nic. He couldn't believe his eyes. "I didn't do this. It wasn't anything like this when I left 16 years ago."

LorEl continued. "Hope is essentially the desire for heaven and the dream of attaining eternal happiness. It is like a cleansing fire that drives away pessimism and lethargy. Its purpose is to light up the hearts of those who have faith in the future, inspiring others to come closer to the Creator, who will lead them to build a sustainable civilization. Come."

Her radiant energies transported Nic once again, this time to another continent. Nic looked down and saw hill after hill covered in cement-block buildings and thriving communities.

"It's Dandora," Nic said excitedly. "But now it covers miles and miles. It was never this big. And the old slum, Mathari Valley, is gone. But how can that be?"

Her arm waved before the scene in front of them, leaving a trail of flames in its path. "It's the result of your hope for the future of Dandora," said LorEl with a smile.

"*My* hope?" Nic looked around at the flourishing city. "I don't understand. I haven't done anything."

"Yes you have, Nic." The angel spoke gently. "The Creator intended for the earth that everything in it is to be shared by all. This is your universal destiny as God's child. Having a fair share of earthly goods is God's intention for every person and every family, for the earth and its resources belong equally to all humanity." The angel continued teaching, "The most important next step for your world is to stop war. The need to end war is easy to understand if you consider the reasons for it. You go to war to get something or to keep what you have. But human nature is not warlike, even though many may think so. It is designed for serving and sharing. Strive for hope for the abolition of war by learning to let go and share."

"But I haven't done anything," Nic repeated, waving his arms in frustration.

"Recognizing the needs of others and acting upon it with hope is a key to ending so much pain and suffering. You have this key," she answered as the flames danced around her form. Her voice strengthened. "My teaching to you is one part of what is called the 'Correcting Time,' a celestial program for correcting centuries of error and darkness on your world. Soon, you will understand. The others will show you more." Her divine fire engulfed Nic. "Sara knows. Listen to her," LorEl roared.

Nic yelled and abruptly sat up in bed drenched in perspiration. Sara awakened startled.

"Nic, what's wrong?"

He grabbed Sara's shoulders. "Is everybody all right Sara? Is anything on fire?" he screamed.

"There's no fire, Nic," Sara said calmly. "Everyone's fine. You had a dream—are you all right?"

Nic calmed down. "Yeah, yeah, I think so. I'm just really hot."

Nic went into the bathroom and leaned on the sink, rinsing his face and neck. The water felt so refreshing. He decided to take a shower to help him cool down. He removed his perspiration-drenched shirt and reached into the shower, turning on a steady stream of water. He stepped back in front of the mirror.

What an amazing dream. Did I really have something to do with the changes I saw?

18

Joy is the serious business of heaven.
—C. S. Lewis

Nic was deep in thought as he reached his hand into the shower to check the water's temperature. Nic noticed that the water failed to warm up and that the pressure of the stream felt stronger than usual. Nic shrugged his shoulders and tried to pull out his hand to remove his shorts before stepping into the shower. But he was unable to retrieve his hand. It was as if the stream was holding his hand in place. He pulled back as hard as he could, leaning his body away from the shower. He couldn't break the hold. He yanked one more time. His yank was answered by a stronger yank from his captor, pulling him into the shower stall underneath the strong flow from the showerhead.

The water became stronger and more powerful. Suddenly, Nic found himself plunging, feet first, down a massive, sunlit, tropical waterfall. He was hurled what felt like hundreds of feet down, the force plunging him deep into a pool of crystal-blue water.

Suspended in the water, Nic opened his eyes and faced a strange being in front of him. The creature was colored a deep blue and composed of a shimmering, circulating energy. The figure resembled a mermaid, her upper body that of a lovely woman, but her lower body a magnificent tail like that of a dolphin. Her lips began to move. Nic could feel vibrations coming to him through the water.

"I am JarEl, the Spirit of Living Water, the Angel of Generosity. Welcome, Nic."

Nic opened his mouth to respond. Air and water flowed from his mouth along with his words. "Welcome to where?" JarEl motioned for him to follow. "Come now with me." She surged upwards towards the light in a torrent of water. Nic tried to keep up with her but struggled.

I'll never make it. I can't hold my breath . . . My breath, my breath, it's gone. Nic felt the warm water flowing in and out of his mouth, throat, and lungs. He was breathing the water! It was so refreshing to him, so pure and cleansing. He looked up and saw a silhouette.

"Hurry Nic."

Nic pulled himself together, finding new strength and comfort. He shot himself up toward the glistening sunlight in the blue sky above. Upon surfacing he saw the angel being further propelled by the stream into the sky. Nic remained below, treading water. "What about me?"

"Swim into the air as if the air were water."

Nic looked at her blankly.

"*Believe*, Nic," she commanded.

Nic closed his eyes to concentrate. Lifting his arms, a sudden gush of water propelled him towards the sky. Together they moved through the atmosphere. JarEl turned to Nic as they hurled through the air with a never-ending flow of water carrying them.

"See, Nic, it's really not that hard once you believe."

Nic gleamed. "Is heaven like this? Will we be able to move through the air like it is water?"

JarEl smiled and looked forward. “Far, far better than this.” She paused for a moment and then continued. “I am here to teach you the art of generosity. Generosity is the essence of love. Always love the Creator with all your heart and soul, Nic, so that one day you will become one with the God who is love. That’s the ultimate goal for each person.”

Nic listened intently, enraptured by his companion.

“Love is more than a feeling or emotion. It is always available directly from the infinite Creator. You cannot create love or hoard it, but your free choices allow the power of love to uplift you as it passes through you to nourish others. Love is the highest form of energy and the most important choice you can ever make. The love that you have expressed during your life transforms your soul, and that’s the only thing humans can bring with them into eternity. The more generous you are, and the more you become perfect in the way that God is perfect, the farther you go.”

“Go where?” asked Nic.

“Upward to higher worlds of light until you reach the abode of the Creator in the Isle of Paradise, at the center of all things.” She smiled.

“So, being generous is the best way to show our love to the Creator?” questioned Nic as they were lifted to the outer part of the earth’s atmosphere.

JarEl continued, “Humans are created to be stewards, to watch over and protect all living things on and in the earth. Especially each other. Watch.”

Nic watched as JarEl stopped, turned, and pointed at the earth. Nic wasn’t aware they had risen so far above the planet.

It is so small, so vulnerable, just sitting there, spinning in the middle of space. Our God is amazing to have made all of this, Nic thought to himself, adjusting to the shock of the view.

"In the beginning, the Creator set in motion a great cosmic event. He sent divine creators out into space from the eternal central universe. Their mission was to catalyze the evolution of seven great superuniverses—vast clusters of galaxies that have slowly but surely evolved billions of inhabited planets, many even more beautiful than your own world."

JarEl then moved her hand as if to hold the Earth in her palm. The Earth began to fade away. Nic reacted by reaching for it to save it from disappearing. JarEL quickly moved Nic further out to deep space to reveal the wonder of the Milky Way. Nick sensed that they were moving back in time, with eons passing him by. JarEL moved her finger and pointed to an empty space in the galaxy. Her finger began to twirl, summoning vast clouds of gasses into being from out of the potency of space, which began to swirl and condense, merging and forming a massive ball of light. As the ball condensed further, it began to throw off matter that soon swung into orbit around it. Nic realized he was witnessing the creation of the solar system.

The clouds around one of the segments of matter dispersed quickly to reveal a fresh, green, and blue Earth with its landmass arranged as it was five billion years ago, merged together as one great supercontinent.

"Creation," whispered Nic in awe. He watched as the land masses slowly moved away from each other, repositioning themselves into the continents and oceans that presently exist.

JarEl brought Nic much closer to the new Earth for a better look. He could see the vegetation and forests growing, and watched as they began to team with wildlife. Everything was alive, and a bewildering variety of species emerged and seemed to march before him in the order of their evolution, leading finally to hominids and primitive humans. Great ancient civilizations emerged. Nic could see Sumerians creating ziggurats and armies of slaves building the Egyptian pyramids. Then he watched the construction of the Great Wall of China, the Roman aqueducts, and the temples of ancient India.

JarEl moved their position close enough to bring these ancient individuals into view, and Nic watched different empires and nations arise and flourish, and then go to war, pillaging each other's property and turning their captives into slaves. JarEl showed him how waves of hatred, starvation, poverty, and desperation dominated the various eras of human life on earth. Then, little by little, the bigger wars subsided and the violence slowly diminished. He watched the rise of towering skyscrapers in great cities and saw lanes of commerce opening across the oceans.

"Listen to this, Nic," said JarEL. She pointed as they descended toward busy Fifth Avenue in New York City. A pedestrian in a business suit nearly tripped over an elderly homeless person in front of an old church. The old man looked up.

"I'm so sorry, sir. Can you help me out?"

Shaking his head, the pedestrian moved on. Nic was surprised that he could hear the thoughts of the bothered pedestrian. "Oh, God. Such misery around here. Why don't you do something about this mess down here? After all, you are God."

A voice came from deep within the businessman that stopped him suddenly.

"I did do something about it. I sent *you*."

The man swallowed with difficulty, turned, and began to slowly walk back to the street person. He bent down to offer him his change and managed to smile at him. JarEl shifted Nic back out to space with a large splash.

"Look." JarEl pointed towards a ray of light coming from the businessman. It was joined by a filament of light shooting forth from the homeless man. Time seemed to speed up, and Nic saw thousands and then millions and then billions of more light rays emanating from the planet. Nic blinked at the splendor.

"They're beautiful. What are they?"

"These subtle energies result from kindness and generosity. They are the energetic result of every human expression of love. They are like prayers that link people to the energies of the Creator. Each act of charity brings the person who receives and the person who gives closer to God, which inspires others, in turn, to spread more love."

Nic noticed rays of light that were larger and wider than the others. "What are those lights?" asked Nic, pointing to them.

"The larger light-forms you see are souls moving on to higher worlds after the death of the body. Your souls are evolving as you grow closer to the Creator, and in the afterlife each soul eventually fuses with the spirit of God that indwells each person. This abiding fragment of God within is a gift from the Creator to all persons—regardless of race or religion."

Nic nodded his head as he tried to understand. "So we truly get closer to the Creator through our loving relationships with each other? Where do we find all the love that's needed? Where is it? Can I show others how to find it?"

JarEl smiled. "Teaching the world to be generous, hopeful, and courageous is the true purpose of the Correcting Time. Being unselfish and charitable is key to ending all the pain and suffering. The energy of generosity wells up within you when you practice stillness each day, when you center yourself in prayer, meditation, and worship. This loving energy wells up and becomes yours just as soon as you let it pour through you in service to others."

Nic felt the ringing truth of JarEl's teaching.

"Nic, continue your lifework of showing forth kindness to others around the world and believe in the power of your sharing. As for your personal life, the Creator has already sent you this key in the form of the woman who is the love of your life. Look into my eyes, and she will come to you."

Nic looked into JarEl's eyes. He saw a trickle of water dripping down her cheek. The trickle quickly turned into raging waters that poured out all over him, sweeping him away. When the water subsided, he found himself on the floor of his shower. He was lying uneasily in a puddle of water as Sara entered the bathroom sleepily and turned on the light.

"Nic, are you okay? Where did all this water come from? Why are you on the shower floor?"

Nic coughed and tried to catch his breath. Sara reached in and turned off the water.

"The water's ice cold. What are you doing? Trying to drown in there?"

"No, no, I'm . . . a little confused."

Sara quickly threw a towel on him and helped him up. Nic was trembling uncontrollably with a frigid chill. "Are you all right?" she exclaimed, noticing his wet shorts.

"Yeah. I'm not too sure what happened, but I do know I'm alright now."

"It sounded like a waterfall in here," said Sara as she wrapped a towel around his shoulders.

"You heard the waterfall? Really?"

Sara looked at him seriously. "What's been happening?"

Nic rubbed his head with the towel. "I'm not too sure. I keep having these dreams." He looked at Sara. Her eyes captured his. "It's you, you're the Angel of Generosity. Her name is JarEl. I knew her face was familiar."

“What are you talking about?” Sara turned to avoid Nic looking further into her eyes. She walked back to the bedroom and got back into bed. “Maybe you should go outside and get a little fresh air.”

Nic curiously looked at Sara as he walked past her. “That’s a good idea. I’ll come to bed in a few minutes.”

“Take your time,” yawned Sara, rolling to her side, her suspicious eyes already closed.

Nic left the room wrapping the towel around himself, still wearing his water-soaked shorts. He stepped outside of the lanai and looked up at the stars. It was a particularly bright night without any moonlight. As Nic stared at the night sky, he noticed a shooting star. Following it with his eyes, he saw a streak of sparkling dust trailing after the moving ball of light. Illumined pieces of dust began to break apart from the uniform dust trail. Nic continued to watch as the scene seemed to get closer and closer. It was aiming right towards him. Nic turned his body to run, but his feet were planted firmly to the ground. The dust reached him and a whirlwind of red, green, and blue crystals encircled him. Nic was frozen.

Those whose minds are shaped by selfless
thoughts give joy when they speak or act.
Joy follows them like a shadow that never leaves them.
—Buddha

Another great angel now appeared before him, this one clothed in whirling clouds, pure white swirls of mist that were constantly in motion, twirling all about her figure. A powerful voice spoke.

"I am RondEl, the Spirit of the Sky and the Angel of Courage."

Nic stiffened, eyes wide, unable to move. White clouds billowed around RondEl's exquisite form.

"Courage is the basis of hope," he bellowed, "the doorway to sublime trust in the mercy of the Creator unseen. True courage is the foundation of faith, and faith makes you receptive to the spirit within you. Nic, you have stepped forward in allegiance to the highest of all duties, the duty to be courageous in faith. And you know that faith is a gift from our Creator."

Nic nodded and looked on in awe.

"Know also, Nic, that every human has profound dignity because they are created in the image of God. Thus, every single man and woman is highly valued by the Creator of the cosmos and by all angelic beings. You possess a personality bestowed by God, irreplaceable in all of eternity. It gives you the freedom to choose your singular path with hope and courage and faith, leading you to a life of love. You must realize that you are vastly more important to the universe than you think. You are much greater than you realize, especially when you share yourself courageously with one another."

The energies of RondEl began to spin around Nic, mesmerizing him with wispy white vapors.

"Most humans never come close to spending the amount of courage they have access to, provided they stand in faith in the loving watchcare of their Creator. Think about it. If you would only let go of your unreasoning fear, so much more courage and fortitude becomes available to you."

The whirlwind turned into a blizzard. Nic still couldn't move his feet. He closed his eyes and covered his head, shielding his face from the showers of tiny crystals now circling about him and forming a vortex of light. When the wind subsided, he removed his hands and opened his eyes. Nic was now on a hilltop, standing next to a red-and-white-striped pole topped with a large shiny glass ball. It was the North Pole marker. Nic leaned forward, looking into the ball. He was amazed to see Santa's workshop reflected inside of it. Everyone was busy moving about. Nic turned to RondEl.

"How can this fairy tale image have anything to do with courage?"

RondEl replied with intensity. "Making the courageous decision to love feeds your faith and inspires you to be ever-more generous. In divine time and as the Creator chooses to respond, all the prayers you offer in faith will surely be answered. Because of God's great gifts to you—especially your indwelling spirit and your irreplaceable personality—you can find the courage to create what you choose to create and love when you choose to love."

Nic was perplexed again. "So there really is a Santa that adults think is a child's fantasy?"

The angel floated slowly around the Pole. "He exists in the sentiments of all good people of faith. He's not believable to the doubters, but he truly does exist for the rest of us. Look for him here." RondEl pointed to Nic's heart.

Nic was flustered. "If people of faith have believed for so long that we can cure the ailments of our world, then why is there still so much suffering?"

RondEl's being expanded with force before Nic's eyes. "All humans face life challenges by their very design. That is how they grow and perfect their souls. When they suffer, it creates an opportunity for others to empathize with them and relieve that suffering, in turn making them more like God who shares all and loves all. When difficult times occur, you spend more time in prayer and rely on the power of the Creator, thus bringing you closer to Him. No prayer goes unheard. Graces are bestowed even when prayers appear to be unanswered. It is the highest joy of every human to recognize the care and concern that the Creator surrounds you with." RondEl paused for a moment as if in deep thought. "Nic, is there any sacrifice you would not suffer for your three children? Would you give your life for them?"

Nic was taken aback. "Of course I would. I would do anything to help and protect them."

"Even if it were unpleasant and painful?" challenged the angel.

"Absolutely," Nic answered confidently.

RondEl smiled. "You nurture them and keep them safe, and you feed and provide for them. You teach them what is right and wrong. You act like they belong to you. But the Creator made you and you belong to the Creator, just as your children, in turn, belong to God. When humans choose to love others as they love themselves—or even better, love their fellows as God loves them—and as they work to alleviate their fellows' suffering, they realize that their own suffering is diminished. Their own burdens are more bearable."

Nic signaled that he agreed.

"All of you are sons and daughters of the living God, and this makes you all siblings to one another all across the nations of the world. Humans can better understand this universal family of God when they nurture their own children in families. Come with me." RondEl waved his billowy arms over Nic's face.

Nic's eyes closed gently as his soul seemed to emerge from deep inside him. He found himself flying over the Pacific Ocean to Asia, passing over Japan and then China. He was now looking down upon the grandeur of Mount Everest, and then descending over a vast landscape and across a seemingly endless desert. Nic then swooped down to the desert's surface and stood upon it. In a flash, he disappeared and became one of its grains of sand. He mingled with the other grains of sand as they were transformed into humans of all races, moving along crowded city streets and farming in the countryside. Before he could focus on his whereabouts, Nic was catapulted back up into space, passing celestial bodies and galaxies. Among the stars, Nic viewed the birth of his children from youngest to oldest. He witnessed the birth of Sara and then his own. He saw his mother gently caressing infant Nic and pressing him to her face. This image of infant with mother dissipated into a fountain of shooting stars.

An all-knowing voice decreed, "I love each one of you more than all of the stars I made that shine for you."

Nic's propulsion through space stopped as the voice echoed in his soul. He was back floating comfortably with RondEl by his side. "But where do I go from here?" he exclaimed, blinking his eyes. "I'm so overwhelmed."

RondEl pointed down to the tiny planet Earth, slowly spinning and suspended in the solar system. "You live in an unprecedented period called the Correcting Time. Never before in the history of all humanity have humans possessed the resources and the ability to begin the eradication of hunger, thirst, and hopelessness among the world's children. There is already enough food being produced today to feed all of the projected populations of tomorrow. There is more than enough medicine and clean water for all if only the people of means had the courage of their convictions. Go, Nic. You are among the messengers who can spread this news."

Nic shook his head. "That's what I've been trying to do, but I haven't been able to. I feel like I have already failed."

RondEl rose above Nic, the swirling of the clouds around him building in intensity. She waved her arms softly, calming them. "What you feel as failure could be true success. You have proved that you have the courage to remain in a state of faith in the Creator, despite your many doubts. Your courage continues to fuel your desire to love others, regardless of your troubles."

The angel stood directly in front of Nic. She leaned her face into his. "Your difficult experiences can help others get through the challenges of their own lives."

The words echoed in Nic's soul. *Where have I heard that before?*

"Nic, go with Sara. Make OSC an extraordinary agency that teaches people how to relieve the terrible suffering of too many of your fellows. Show folks how they can end all the deprivation and inequality by courageously spreading the love of the Creator to those less fortunate. Proclaim the message you are destined to deliver to humanity. Your own spirit of sharing will spark a new spirit of generosity around the world."

Before Nic could get in a word, RondEl's clouds whirled over him and disappeared. Nic was returned to the comfort of his bed, sleeping soundly. Sara rolled over to face Nic. She smiled as she softly pulled the blanket up over his shoulder. "How are you feeling?" she asked sweetly. "Are you all right?"

Nic blinked his eyes open. There she was, his special Sara. Nic always felt that there was something exceptional about her, and now he felt it more than ever.

Nic sat up slowly, his head still whirling with the angels' revelations. Sara snuggled up next to him, sitting quietly. Nic finally broke the silence. "You know what just happened to me, don't you?" asked Nic as he placed his hand on hers.

Sara turned her head to look at Nic, cracking a mischievous smile. "Tell me about it."

Nic straightened up a little bit more as he arched his back, enjoying the stretch. "I have a feeling that you could tell me more about what has been going on than I can."

"Why would you think that?"

Nic caught a glimpse of that familiar sparkle in her eyes. "You are the help that I've been asking for, aren't you?" asked Nic. "You've known the answers from the beginning. That's why they always tell me to listen to you." Nic hung his head as if he was embarrassed by his ignorance.

Sara placed her hand under his chin and gently lifted his head. "Tell me what you've learned."

"Tonight the angels showed me that the spirit of sharing isn't just about the action of giving," Nic explained with excitement.

"It is about the Creator dwelling inside each one of us who makes His infinite love available to us in deep stillness and contemplation and when we are generous to others. We are the children of the same Creator, which makes us all brothers and sisters. When we go within and connect with this loving spirit, we are compelled to help our brothers and sisters and share the love that is flowing through us. That truly is the will of the Creator. Together, we can be hopeful, generous, and courageous. Together, we can end the pain and suffering." Nic nodded his head. "I'm getting it, Sara. I believe we can do it."

Sara reached over and pressed her hand firmly on to his chest. "I have always believed in you, Nic. Always."

Nic looked at her hand on his chest and then raised his head. As their eyes met, Nic's eyes widened.

"Yes, Nic. I believed in you since we first met. After all, you are Santa Claus."

"You knew that I gave you the coat," Nic said, still being embraced with her eyes.

Sara nodded slowly.

"But how did it get to your bedroom? I didn't take it to you. It was in my room, under my bed."

"You believed. Anything is possible if you just have faith." Sara chuckled. "Like I said, Nic, you are Santa Claus."

A tear pooled in Nic's eyes as he remembered his mother telling him that she felt he was destined to be a great gift bearer like Saint Nicholas and that if he worked hard enough, he could grow up to be Santa Claus.

"I was happy to agree to fulfill my mission with you. I knew that, together, we could really make a difference."

"Your mission?" Nic blinked the wetness from his eyes. "You have a mission too?"

"The same one as you, silly," said Sara happily. "Nicholas told Mother Spirit and Michael that our common mission was of greater magnitude and it would need to be fulfilled together."

Nic's mind locked. Sara's words completely surprised him. She just mentioned Nicholas and Michael. He thought he was the only one who knew about them. What else does she know?

Spiritual growth yields lasting joy,
peace which passes all understanding.
—The Urantia Book

"Wait. You know about Nicholas and Michael? And who is this being you call 'Mother Spirit'?"

Sara turned to face Nic, crossing her legs and getting comfortable as if she was settling in to tell her kids a story.

"Mother Spirit is like an angel, but so very much more," she said fondly. "She has been instrumental in bringing us together."

That must be the third figure I saw in the fire when we met in Africa. That's who Sara calls Mother Spirit.

"She has always been with me," continued Sara. "Mother is who I feel in my spirit and who guides me. We talk all the time. I don't know what I would do without her."

"You talk all the time? I only see Michael every now and then. He says he's always with me, but I don't see him very often," Nic said as if disappointed.

"You don't have to see him to talk to him, Nic. Their spirit is always inside of you, just like the indwelling spirit gifted to you from the Creator. You just have to be still and listen." Sara punched Nic gently on his shoulder. "You've been so busy worrying about money, donations, and your board of directors that you haven't taken the time to be still and listen."

Nic took in a deep breath. "You're right, Sara." He swung his legs over the side of the bed. He looked over his shoulder with his forehead furrowed. "So if you knew about all of this from the beginning, why didn't you tell me?"

"You *were* told, several times by Michael and by me, but you didn't get it. You were too busy trying to force things to happen instead of calming your mind long enough to receive guidance. You forgot that your indwelling spirit could lead you to fulfill your mission far better than any of your worldly ideas. Remember, Nic, that you were chosen because of your special giving and sharing spirit, but you didn't believe in your gifts enough to make things happen according to the power of God. How often have you taken the time to quiet your busy mind and receive the Creator's love in your heart?" Sara scooted across the bed and sat next to Nic. "But no matter what happened, your faith remained and you persisted in the face of adversity."

"You still could have told me, instead of letting me make a fool out of myself," said Nic, leaning into Sara.

Sara hooked her arm around Nic's and gave it a tug. "In order for you to fulfill the mission, your understanding needed to come from within your own experience. You had to realize it yourself, even it if it did take fire, water, and wind to do so."

Nic laughed. "Nicholas and Michael didn't know what they were getting into when they picked me, did they?"

"Actually, they did," said Sara. "That's why they asked me to help and encourage you through it all."

"So you really are my angel." Nic leaned into Sara and rested his head on hers. "That's why I've always thought about you and felt you throughout the years. We are true soul mates."

Sara turned towards Nic, kissing him softly on the cheek. "Yes, my love, we truly are."

"I guess Mother Spirit never had to take *you* on a crazy adventure through time and space to knock some sense into you," Nic said with a sarcastic tone.

"Actually, she did," confessed Sara.

Nic sat up straight. "Seriously? She did?"

"I've always believed in you. I never once doubted the sharing spirit within you and your ability to fulfill your mission, but sometimes . . ." Sara paused, choosing her words before continuing.

"Sometimes what? Go ahead," prodded Nic.

"Sometimes you were so stubborn and foolish, it seemed like you were never going to get it. I was getting impatient, so I asked Mother Spirit if I could see the results of our mission."

"She showed you?" Nic's voice quivered.

"She showed me what happens when the spirit of sharing is put into action."

Nic's mind ran wild with images of what he thought that could be. He pictured communities sharing surplus medicines and supplies, a global relief monitoring system, and groups providing the knowledge and tools needed to allow societies to grow their own food and live sustainably and peacefully.

"What was it like, Sara? What did she show you? Can you tell me?"

Sara sat quietly. Nic noticed her eyes were closed. "No, I can't tell you," she said calmly as she opened her eyes. Nic frowned.

"I was afraid of that," he scowled.

Sara stood and reached for Nic's hand. "I can show you."

Nic looked up at Sara. She smiled and nodded. Nic reached for her hand as he stood slowly, trembling.

"You have proven yourself, Nic. Mother Spirit will allow you to see what will happen as a result of your continued hope, generosity, and courage. But first, you have to..."

"Believe," said Nic. "I have to still my busy mind and look inside myself, listen to the guidance, and believe in my spirit of sharing."

Sara smiled. "I believe in you, Nic."

Nic squeezed Sara's hand gently. "So do I."

Sara closed her eyes and took a deep breath. Nic joined her, closing his eyes breathing deeply. The rhythm of their breath was in sync as it slowed, their inhales deepening. Nic felt his mind calm, focusing on his spirit within. Sara's voice interrupted his stillness.

"Open your eyes, Nic."

What he saw was beyond his wildest dreams. Nic and Sara stood on a small flat clearing on top of a mountain peak with an expansive view.

"What is all of this?" asked Nic as he spun around, looking all around him.

"What you see is the result of your hope, generosity, and courage," said a strong female voice.

Nic quickly looked at Sara. She shrugged her shoulders as if she was saying, "I didn't say anything."

Nic continued to turn around. Behind him stood a radiantly beautiful woman, a divine being glowing with a gentle yet vibrant spirit. She smiled at Nic. Her accepting and welcoming eyes shined with a familiar sparkle. He turned to look at Sara, her eyes emitting the same sparkle, the glistening he had seen in her eyes so many times.

"This is Mother Spirit," said Sara, motioning towards the lovely presence.

"I feel like I've known you all my life," Nic found himself saying slowly.

"You've looked into my eyes many times," cooed Mother Spirit. "And I have come to you in many forms and images." She held her arms up in the air as she stepped around Nic. "This is what happens when selfishness is replaced with sharing, when the well-being of others and of the planet is made a priority." She stepped to the edge of the mountain. "Come, Nic. Come and see."

Nic took Sara's hand, and they joined Mother Spirit at the edge of the mountain. Hearing the roar of flowing water, Nic looked down. Forceful waterfalls streamed from springs in the side of the mountain, the water surging majestically to the base of the mountain, forming rivers that gushed into the vastness below. His eyes followed one of the rushing rivers that snaked away from the mountain toward a large desert. The rolling waters branched into canals that spread out into a vast agricultural area. Massive panels hung over the vegetation, moving methodically like sheets blowing in the wind, collecting the hydrogen and oxygen in the air, creating a mist that watered the rows of crops below. Nic's eyes were wide, amazed by what he saw.

"I've seen that technology before," exclaimed Nick. "The panels emit energy that sparks the hydrogen and oxygen, creating water." Nic tugged on Sara's arm. "Sara, desert communities can grow their own food. Nobody has to go hungry. They can provide for themselves. They don't have to struggle or go to war for their necessities." Nic continued to tug on Sara's arm. Sara giggled. He reminded her of their boys tugging on her arm when they saw a toy that they really wanted.

Nic took a few steps back, still holding tight to Sara's hand. Mother Spirit stood by Sara's side, smiling on them both.

Stumbling, Nic turned to his right, Sara's grip stopping him from falling. What he saw on this side of the mountain was even more astounding. The dry desert morphed into the spacious landscape of the northern polar ice region. The stars of the Milky Way shone brightly in the dark sky above a snow-covered, treeless plain. An odd reflection of these stars glistened on the metallic surface of massive inverted funnels collecting the methane gas released from the melting ice. Nic marveled that these devices were hovering over large holes that were emitting methane gas. The gas was collected by these massive caps and routed to generators that powered glass-enclosed greenhouses. Nic squinted, trying to see more clearly, but the rotating multi-colored LED lights in the massive greenhouse made it difficult for him to see what was being grown in the hydroponic systems.

"From one extreme to another," pondered Nic. "Food grown in the hot desert, now vegetation in a frozen tundra. Amazing."

Mother Spirit stood close to Sara. Nic noticed that she hadn't left her side. "All of this is possible?" Nic asked her, pointing to the technology below.

"When people come together who share a passion and have a common goal, anything is possible. That is, if they organize themselves according to the three key values of social sustainability." Mother Spirit turned and looked directly at Nic and continued. "Remember, Nic, what Archangel Michael taught you. These values work together like the three legs of a stool. As he told you, the universal core values are life, equality, and growth. How do we create a socially and environmentally sustainable village, city, nation, or planet? How do we prevent warfare, exploitation, and the rise and fall of whole civilizations? It is only possible when technologies and social systems are based on these higher values. They have to be present together if a civilization is to sustain itself over centuries and millennia. Everyone must have the opportunity and resources needed for abundant life and growth."

Nic listened and drank in Mother's words, with tears in his eyes.

"You are looking at the result of a society whose leaders have honored this great truth. Social sustainability is well-understood and fully implemented in all of the advanced inhabited worlds in my vast domains."

Mother Spirit took Sara's small hand and gently led her to the other side of the mountain. Nic followed. Finding comfort with his hand in Sara's, he didn't dare let go. It was as if he was a small boy and he needed to hold on to her hand to feel safe.

They stood hand in hand, overlooking the other side of the mountain.

"It's the African plains," whispered Nic, recognizing the mountains and the terrain. He looked around purposefully as if searching for something.

"What are you looking for?" asked Sara, noticing his behavior.

"It's nothing," laughed Nic, realizing it was silly to think that he'd see the half-buried abandoned Land Rover from his adventures years ago. He surveyed the area one more time. He didn't see the vehicle, but he did see several bamboo towers. Nic pointed to a hillside. "Do you know what those are?" Nic had forgotten that Sara had already been on the mountain and knew what was before them. Sara shook her head, allowing the excitement of the teacher inside of Nic to instruct her. "Those are Water-trees. I have read about these structures." Nic took a couple of steps forward as if to get a closer look. "A bamboo frame supports a mesh polyester material inside. Water vapor condenses on the cold surface of the mesh, forming drops of water. The water trickles down into a reservoir at the bottom. The community now has access to clean drinking water. No more walking for miles to collect water that is too often polluted and unsafe for drinking." Nic marveled at the cleverness of the canopy that shaded the collected water so that it would not evaporate.

The rumbling of a waterfall just below him caught Nic's attention. He followed its flow to the base of the mountain. The river it created curved to the left, rippling past a large pond teeming with fish. The aquaponic farm was simple and contained, allowing the raising of both fish and vegetables. Just past the farm was a large machine that looked similar to an old train engine.

"What are they doing?" asked Nic as he watched people throwing bags into the back of the structure.

It was Sara's turn to teach Nic. "This is a new type of anaerobic digester, which has the capability of converting refuse of all kinds into fertilizer and compost for farming. It is also capable of converting it into methane gas that can be used to generate electricity."

Nic didn't know what to say. He tilted his head back, looking up at the sky, his mind swimming with what he had seen. His racing thoughts were interrupted by a strange object above the mountain.

"What is that?" questioned Nic as he tugged on Sara's arm, directing her gaze to the sky. "It looks like a huge spider web."

Mother Spirit pointed to the object. "It is a highly sophisticated ionized carbon nanotube web that has been placed in the atmosphere between the sun and earth. The web is held by drones which are programmed to adjust the amount of heat that passes through onto different regions of the earth."

Nic couldn't believe his eyes. His crazy idea for dealing with climate change and extreme weather situations had been put into place. "The nanotube web acts like an adjustable sun shade," Nic explained proudly as he continued to tug on Sara's arm. Sara giggled. He reminded her of their boys tugging on her arm when they saw a toy that excited them. "This technology is designed to expand and contract according to desired filter levels. It can regulate the amount of heat a region receives from the sun, stabilizing extreme temperatures. Nic paused for a moment to marvel at the impressive structure. "Just by shading the oceans one day at a time," continued Nic, "the temperatures can be reduced and devastating storms that thrive on warm water temperatures can be controlled. Coral reefs can repair themselves and massive algae blooms reduced. The solar web can even stop the disintegration of the polar ice caps and grow them back to stabilized levels."

Nic paused again, his eyes fixed on the web.

"That's amazing," marveled Nic. He took a few steps back. The trio, now hand-in-hand, stood quietly as they stared onto the scene before them. "This is like my dreams come true," sighed Nic, blinking away a tear from his eye. "It's more than I could ever hope for."

"This *is* your dream come true, Nic."

Nic felt a squeeze on his free hand.

"And the result of your hope," added another familiar voice.

Nic looked to his right. Michael and Nicolas stood hand-in-hand next to him. The power and love on both sides of Nic filled his spirit.

"Is this all real, or am I dreaming?" Nic hoped it was real, but he just couldn't believe it.

"This is the reality of a just society that promotes the well-being of each person's physical, environmental, and economic condition, where the citizens embody courage, generosity, and hope," explained Michael.

Nicholas stepped around Michael and stood behind Nic, placing his hands on his shoulders. "You were chosen for this mission because you deeply believe in the true spirit of Santa Claus, the spirit of sharing. You recognize that there is much more to giving than material gifts. You see the importance of the gift of dignity and the ability to take care of one's self and one's neighbor in a civilization in which the Golden Rule truly does rule." Nicholas pointed past Nic. "What you see before you is the gift of social sustainability that you will help give the world through your efforts with OSC."

Nic was speechless.

Mother Spirit circled in front of Sara and Nic. "Nic, do you remember when you told Sara you weren't doing enough?"

Nic nodded his head. He clearly remembered that day and the failure that he felt.

"Everything that you have done that you regard as insignificant was monumental, each in its own way. Your efforts have proved to be the cause for all that you see." Mother Spirit stepped closer to Nic. "This is a key part of the Correcting Time. You will succeed as long as you believe in the power of our loving Creator."

Nic broke the chain and stepped forward, shaking his head. He still couldn't believe it. "But how can the small things that I do result in all of this?"

"We will show you. Close your eyes, Nic," whispered Sara.

Nic knew what that meant. He was about to take another exciting journey. Nic closed his eyes as his mind raced, trying to guess his destination. "Where are we going?" He finally asked.

"India," said Michael.

Nic kept his eyes closed tightly. "Why? LorEl took me to Gomoh not long ago." His tone portrayed disappointment. He was hoping for a new, grand experience.

"Open your eyes." Sara once again whispered the instructions.

A large gated fence stood directly in front of him.

"Where are we now?" Nick whispered back.

The building behind the fence was vaguely familiar. The large structure had a grand double-door entrance framed by two intricately carved stone urns. One side of the door opened, revealing a woman holding a neatly swaddled infant in her arms. She followed the sidewalk that led to the gate across the short courtyard. She approached the gate, opening it for the guests.

The scene stirred a memory for Nic. "I think I've been here," he said softly to the woman. He looked behind her at the large modern building. It seemed familiar to him, but the grandeur told him that it was not the same place.

The woman smiled. She walked closer to Nic, handing the sleeping infant towards him. Understanding her offer, he held out his arms and reached for the baby. He cradled her gently as he gazed at her sweet face.

"I don't understand," he said as his attention turned towards the others. "Why are we here?"

"An infant was found abandoned," explained the woman. "A young man's caring spirit led him to help her, and he brought her here. Because of his generosity, the child had the opportunity to live a wonderful life."

Sara gently caressed the infant's face with her fingers. "This woman not only runs this orphanage," said Sara, nodding towards the woman, "but she has also set up programs throughout the area that assist communities with growing their own food, making clean water, and arriving at decisions that support their sustainability. Programs much like the ones you saw from the mountaintop."

"Your spirit of sharing has made her efforts possible," said Nicolas as he stepped behind Nic. He took off his red cloak and placed it royally around Nic's shoulders. Nic looked down at the red flowing velvet draping down his arms. "When you do things with hope and courage and in the spirit of sharing," Nicholas said softly, "you feel something moving in you. You feel maximum joy."

"Nicholas!" Nic couldn't say anything else. The supreme joy that he felt embrace his spirit was overwhelming.

The woman stepped forward and looked deeply into Nic's eyes.

"I feel like I know you," Nic finally said as he studied her face.

The woman took the baby from Nic and caressed her lovingly. "Many years ago, you found a baby in these streets just like this and brought her to this orphanage. She was taken well care of and as she grew, she thanked God for her life and the opportunities that were given to her." She stroked the majestic cloak draping over Nic's arm. "At Christmas, gifts were often donated for the children in the orphanage with tags signed by Santa Claus. Out of all of the gifts that she received, this girl reveled in the one gift that she knew was given to her by the real Santa Claus."

Nic continued to study her face, mesmerized by her words.

"You gave me a precious gift many years ago," the woman said to Nic. "Because of this gift, I have felt the desire to spread the spirit of sharing and to help others."

Nic's eyes widened.

"I am that baby that you rescued from the street," she revealed with a smile. "You, Santa Claus, gave me the gift of life."

We live in an unprecedented time.
Never before in the history of humankind have we
possessed the ability to end so much suffering,
to become a part of the [illegible] to
[illegible] the spirit of [illegible]

[illegible]

[illegible]

* * *

Learn more about [illegible]
[illegible]